Horsefeathers

Horse Angels

Dandi Daley Mackall

CPH.
SAINT LOUIS

Horsefeathers

Horsefeathers!
Horse Cents
Horse Whispers in the Air
A Horse of a Different Color
Horse Angels
Home Is Where Your Horse Is

Interest level: ages 12–16

All Scripture quotations are taken from the HOLY BIBLE, NEW INTERNATIONAL VERSION®. NIV®. Copyright © 1973, 1978, 1984 by International Bible Society. Used by permission of Zondervan Publishing House. All rights reserved.

Text copyright © 2000 Dandi Daley Mackall
Published by Concordia Publishing House
3558 S. Jefferson Avenue, St. Louis, MO 63118-3968
Manufactured in the United States of America

Library of Congress Cataloging-in-Publication Data

Mackall, Dandi Daley.
   Horse ANGELS / Dandi Daley Mackall.
     p.   cm. — (Horsefeathers)
Summary: Scoop prays that God will keep her horses safe, solve her friend Jen's health problems, and make a wild horse trust people again.
   ISBN 0-570-07086-4
   [1. Horses—Fiction. 2. Christian life—Fiction.] I. Title.
   PZ7.M1905 Hm 2000
   [Fic]—dc21
                                  00-010383

1 2 3 4 5 6 7 8 9 10   09 08 07 06 05 04 03 02 01 00

This book is dedicated to Dan,

the son I never thought I'd have

(but I'm glad I do!).

Scoop! Dotty! Scoop! Dotty! Scoop! Dotty!"
I squeezed my eyes shut and tried to ignore
my brother's shouts. The cries pierced down
through the holes in our roof, dangling there like
icicles above my throbbing head.

I'd just clicked off the living room lamps and
plopped down on the couch so hard dust clouds
puffed up and made me cough. That fast I'd dozed
off when B.C. started yelling from the rooftop.

"Scoop! Dotty!" Louder now, the chant
hung in the cold, Halloween wind, sounding
more like *Scoopdoddy, scoopdoddy, scoopdoddy!*

Dotty shuffled in from the kitchen and
clicked on the ceramic dog-lamp's nose. "Ain't
that B.C. hollering?" she asked, wiping her hands
on her slick, black pants. Pale light washed over
her face and reflected off her thick-lensed glasses.
My aunt's shadow on the faded green wall looked
like a dark snowman.

I groaned. "Probably another trick-or-treater.
I told B.C. to stay off the roof so he could hand
out the candy."

The *Scoopdoddies* hadn't let up. I heard a *thump*—B.C. jumping down from the roof. Then the door flung open, setting off a wave of pinpricks through my skull.

"Scoop! Didn't you hear me?" he demanded. B.C. grabbed my arm and yanked. He's the smallest kid in fourth grade, five years behind me, but he almost pulled me off the couch. "I saw *fire!*" he screamed.

"Horsefeathers, B.C.!" I said, jerking my arm back. "It's probably lightning or something."

Dotty crossed the room and stared out the front door. "Scoop?" Her voice was hushed, and somehow that scared me more than all of B.C.'s screaming.

I sat up too fast. The pain in my head blurred and swirled behind my eyes. "Is it really a fire?" I asked.

"Oh Lord, please," Dotty said, not answering me. She whirled from the door. "Scoop, you better—"

But I was already racing to the door. I felt like I'd swallowed an icicle that made my bones shiver.

Dotty was at the phone, dialing. "Hello! We got us a fire at—"

I ran outside and saw bright yellow flames grabbing at the black sky. The flames were coming from Horsefeathers.

2

In a blind panic I ran as fast as I could toward the flames, toward my stable, toward my horse. I tried to pray, to plead with God to keep Orphan safe. In my mind, as I tore down our driveway, I could see my mare, black as charcoal, the horse I'd adopted the day my parents had adopted me. What if Orphan got trapped in the barn? What if the horses couldn't get out? Why hadn't I stayed at the barn and guarded them?

I passed a lady with two kids dressed like pumpkins. They were pointing toward Horsefeathers and the fire that rose toward the moon. "I wanna see the fire!" cried one of the pumpkins.

My heart pounded. I was gasping and swallowing tears as I came to Horsefeathers Lane. Flames lapped the back of the barn like giant snake tongues. A few people leaned over the paddock fence watching. Someone shouted my name.

Without slowing, I climbed the fence and jumped down, falling in the dirt. Somebody

7

clasped my elbow and helped me to my feet. It was Travis Zucker, Jen's older brother, and he was pulling the barn hose behind him.

"Take it easy," Travis said, his voice deep. "It's not the barn. Somebody set fire—"

I missed the rest because I had to see for myself. I scurried around to the back of the barn. A few feet from the barn door, fire danced from three bales of hay. Sparks flew dangerously close to the barn roof, then whisked to the west.

Tears rolled down my cheeks. *Thank You, God,* I prayed. Only the hay bales were burning. Not Horsefeathers. Not horses.

I felt Travis behind me and heard the spitting of the hose as water spurted from the nozzle. Travis aimed the long hose at the barn, then at the bales.

"Travis," I yelled, "where's—?"

"Orphan's over there," he answered. "She's fine, Scoop."

I took a step toward the west pasture, where Travis pointed, and saw my horse. A rush of relief filled my chest until I thought I might burst. Still, I wanted to feel Orphan for myself. I needed to touch her, to know she was safe.

But the other horses were my responsibility too. "How about the rest of the horses?" I asked.

"Angel and Ham are in the barn." Travis moved closer to the fire, dragging the hose with him. "I was coming down to check on Angel when I saw smoke. I tried to get all the horses out, but those two wouldn't budge. The fire's not going anywhere though. The wind's blowing in the right direction."

Sirens blared in the distance, growing louder. The first fire truck pulled into Horsefeathers Lane.

"Go on," Travis said, reading my mind that I had to see Orphan.

I smiled my thanks and ran through the paddock. Maggie's old white mare, Moby, stood next to Orphan. They whinnied a welcome at me. Orphan stuck her beautiful head over the fence, and I threw my arms around her neck. Her horsey smell mingled with smoke. In the dark, she looked blacker than midnight.

I cried into her soft, fuzzy neck and thanked God for keeping her safe. Why hadn't I camped out at the barn? I should have stayed with Orphan. On Halloween night, anything could happen. I should have known.

"I'm sorry, girls," I told the horses, stroking Moby too. "Where's Cheyenne?" Cheyenne is Jen Zucker's Paint mare. Her dad pays me to keep the Paint at Horsefeathers and make sure she gets hard workouts so she won't be too feisty for the Zucker kids. Cheyenne should have been hanging out with Moby and Orphan.

I cupped my hands and yelled out to the pasture. "Cheyenne! Here girl!" I whistled for her.

Orphan nickered, but there was no sign of the Paint.

I left the mares and joined Travis and the fire fighters. The blaze had died down, leaving smoldering, black rectangles, like giant blocks of coal.

Dotty was talking to the tallest, skinniest firefighter I'd ever seen. From a distance, they might have been a telephone pole and a fence post. My aunt, who is barely five feet tall in the oxfords she wears to work at the grocery store, had to look straight up to have eye contact with the firefighter. A Haflinger Austrian pony looking up to a lean, streamlined Standard Bred— that's what they'd have been if they'd been horses.

"Well, I'm right sorry to make you miss your daughter's birthday party," Dotty was saying to the firefighter.

She jerked her head toward me. "Scoop! Everything okay?"

B.C. ran up behind me. "Told you!" he shouted. "Told you I saw fire!" He stopped and seemed to see the charred hay bales for the first time. Quicker than a horsefly, his mood switched. He ran to Dotty and wrapped his arms as far as they'd go around her broad waist, burying his head against her. "I want to go home!" he cried. "Now!"

"It's all right, B.C. Hon," Dotty said, trying to pry his head away from her stomach. "Look how Jesus kept Horsefeathers safe! Thank You, Lord. Thank you, sir," she told the firefighter, as if Jesus and this firefighter were shoulder to shoulder and she could see them both. "And Travis, ain't you the hero!"

"NOW!" B.C. demanded.

The firefighters stopped talking and stared at my trembling brother, who still clung to my aunt. He looked like a baby kangaroo stuck in his mama's pouch. Since our folks died when B.C. was just 2 years old, Dotty's been the only mama he remembers.

"I reckon we'll get along home," Dotty said. Then, with B.C. still attached, she shuffled them off to her car.

The firefighter who had been talking to Travis nodded at me. Travis said something to him I couldn't hear, and the man, his helmet tucked under his arm, strolled over and held out his hand.

I shook it. "Thanks," I said, sounding stupid.

He smiled at me. "You don't recognize me, do you?"

I stared at his gray coveralls and his leathery face, his forehead rimmed by an invisible band where his hat had been. He looked kind of familiar, but I didn't know why. I shook my head.

"Wade Wilson. From church?"

I *had* seen him, just not dressed like a firefighter. He sang in church sometimes—in a suit and tie. "I'm sorry. You sing." It came out stupid again, like I was sorry that he sang. I could feel Travis watching and listening. Why were people so much harder to talk to than horses?

"I'm on the volunteer fire brigade. Lots of regulars are out tonight—probably trick-or-treating with their kids." He nodded toward the smoking hay bales. "Looks like somebody went in for the *tricks*."

"Scoop! What happened? Is everybody okay? Where's Moby? We saw the fire and I knew it was Horsefeathers Stable and we came as fast as we could, and if anything has happened to Moby, I'll never ever forgive myself!" Maggie 37 Brown made her dramatic entry and barely stopped long enough to catch her breath. She was dressed in a long, red gown and looked like an English Queen, complete with a crown and a golden scepter. She was surrounded by two kings, a court jester, the seven and nine of hearts, and two fuzzy white mice. I recognized Bryan and Matt and Alison from high school.

Travis took Maggie's hand and bowed. "Queen Maggie 37 *Red* perhaps?" Maggie's real last name is Brown, but she changes her "stage name" to match the color of her clothes. The "37" is real though, her actual middle name.

Travis was teasing Maggie, but I could see real terror in her eyes, and I felt like it was my fault.

"Moby's fine," I assured her. "All the horses are fine." Then I remembered Cheyenne. "Travis, have you seen Chey? She wasn't out to pasture with Moby and Orphan, and she didn't come when I called her. Are you sure she's not still in the barn?"

"I don't think so," Travis said.

I walked to the barn, and Travis and Queen Maggie followed. Ham, officially named Buckingham's British Pride, stamped in his stall, pawing the ground.

"Somebody ought to call Carla before she hears about the fire from someone else," Maggie said.

Maggie was right. Carla Buckingham boarded Ham at Horsefeathers and helped me as much as Maggie and Jen did. How was I going to tell her how close we'd come to disaster? My head hurt thinking about what I'd say. It was like, with the crisis over, my brain remembered I had a headache, and it went back to throbbing.

Maggie's costumed friends followed her around like loyal subjects. One of the mice had a cell phone in her car, and Maggie left to call Carla.

I took a second to scratch Ham's jaw to calm him down a bit. "Where's Jen?" I asked Travis.

"She's sleeping. I think she's coming down with something—again." Travis' Appaloosa,

Angel, kept eating hay in the next stall, as if he couldn't care less about fires. I liked the way Travis stroked Angel's neck and withers and whispered to him.

It only took a minute to see that Cheyenne wasn't in the barn. "Where could she be?" I asked, thinking out loud. I could get Orphan and search the back pastures. But if Cheyenne had been out in the pasture, why wouldn't she come when I called her?

Maggie stuck her head inside the barn. "Scoop! You better hear this!"

I jogged back to the paddock, scared of what could be wrong now. Sheriff Orville stood in the middle of the firefighters. He pushed his white cowboy hat away from his brow. "You lose a horse?" he asked me.

"I may have," I said.

"This one's real pretty—spotted—but wild as can be." The sheriff shook his head. "We can't catch it."

"That's got to be Cheyenne," Travis said. "She probably got spooked and jumped the fence."

"Come on," said the sheriff. "I'll take you."

I ran to the barn and got a coffee can of oats and a lead rope. Then Travis and I hopped in the back seat of the squad car.

Gravel spit as Sheriff Orville backed out and headed down the lane. I looked over my shoulder at Horsefeathers Stable, split into squares by the metal bars over the car windows.

Travis sighed. "Wade, the fireman, said if the bales had been six inches closer to the barn, or the wind just a degree stronger, the whole barn would have burned down."

I stared at that barn and shivered as it grew smaller, leaving nothing in the blackness but still-rising smoke. Fear in the pit of my stomach seeped up to my brain, flooding me with *what if* questions. What if Horsefeathers had burned down? What if Orphan had been inside? What if whoever did this came back?

3

"There she is!" Sheriff Orville swerved to the side of the road so fast, I ended up in Travis' lap. I tried to push myself away without looking at him.

Our patrol car pulled up behind another police car.

I glanced out the front window just in time to see hooves. Cheyenne jumped over the hood of the car, clearing it a foot.

"There she goes! Look out!" yelled the sheriff.

Travis struggled with the back door, but the sheriff had to open it from the outside. We piled out into thick weeds and brush. I could see by the bright three-quarter moon directly overhead that we were by the railroad tracks, almost a mile past the cemetery.

"I can't believe that horse!" Travis exclaimed.

Two deputies strolled up to us from the other car. One had a bushy mustache that hid everything from his nose down. The other one didn't look much older than Travis. They were highway patrol, dressed in khaki pants and blue-gray jackets with emblems on the front. I didn't think I'd ever seen them before.

"We can't get near her," said the mustached man. If he'd been a horse, he might have been a Morgan—stocky and dependable. "We stuck around to keep an eye on her, but I can't see how you think to catch her."

"She's dangerous," said the young patrol-man, his greenish eyes showing white all around the rims. He kept shifting his weight from one foot to the other, like one of the Dalton horses that got shut up too long. "Don't get too close to that wild animal! She was *this* close to kicking me!" he said and held up his thumb and forefinger to show us how close he'd come to extinction.

"I need to go to her alone," I said.

"Well, little lady," said Sheriff Orville, "I don't know about that."

"The horse knows Scoop," Travis explained. "Cheyenne trusts her." Travis is like a perfect Palomino—blond, like all the Zuckers—with twice as many muscles as the police officers. He says my voice makes horses trust me. *His* deep, calm voice has the same effect on people.

The sheriff twisted his mouth sideways, then nodded.

"Go on, Scoop," Travis said. "I'll follow you."

I nodded and started toward the field, where Cheyenne stood like a wild stallion, her tail lifted high and her neck arched against the backdrop of sky and stars. She looked amazing, like a painting.

"Easy, Cheyenne," I called, trying to sound like I did every day when I rode her. But my voice shook, and the cold wind stabbed my head like the blade of a knife. I held out the can of oats, half-empty from the ride in the squad car. "Let's go home, Chey."

I'd forgotten about the lead rope, still in my hand. Without looking back, I tossed the rope behind me, hoping Travis would see and have it ready when I needed it. "Look, Cheyenne," I said, stepping steadily closer to her. "No hands!"

Cheyenne snorted, then pawed the ground.

I put my arms out at my sides, like airplane wings, and kept muttering a stream of nonsense as I closed the distance between us, moving in at a 45-degree angle. Cheyenne tossed her head and reared, just a couple of inches off the ground.

Behind me one of the deputies hollered something, but I ignored him. I stayed to one side of Cheyenne, where she could see me. Horses see great everywhere except directly in front or in back of them, and Cheyenne didn't need any more surprises.

Closer and closer I inched. She was almost within reach.

Suddenly the horse reared. I hadn't seen it coming. My feet tangled. I stumbled and fell backwards on the hard ground. Cheyenne pawed the air. I felt the breeze of her hooves as I scooched backwards in the dirt on my elbows.

I froze. I knew I was dead center in front of her, in the danger zone between her lines of vision. But I couldn't move.

Travis cried out behind me. I heard his footsteps getting closer.

"Get!" I yelled to Cheyenne. "Shoo! Haw!"

Cheyenne's eyes glowed white with fear. Her front hooves hit the ground. She pivoted and galloped off.

Travis knelt beside me. "Are you okay? Did she hurt you?"

"Yes," I said. "I mean yes, I'm okay. She didn't hurt me." Tears blurred my eyes and made my aching head swim as I let Travis help me to my feet. "Travis," I said, trying not to cry, "what did I do? I can't believe I yelled at her."

"Scoop," Travis said, brushing off my back, "you had to. If she—"

"No!" I cried. "If I'd just stayed calm, we would have had her, Travis. Now I've ruined her. She'll never trust me." I took a step and felt dizzy, stopped, and took another step. I felt Travis next to me. "I'm going after her, Travis," I said.

"Hey, is the girl all right?" shouted one of the deputies.

"Scoop," Travis said softly, putting his arm around my waist, "maybe you should go back with them. I'll keep after Cheyenne."

"I'm okay," I insisted. "Really, Travis, I'm not going back without Cheyenne. Tell them."

Travis started to say something, then took in a long, deep breath and turned back to the deputies. "Yeah, she's okay! We're going after the horse. You might as well go back. Thanks!"

The younger deputy waved, not offering any argument. I heard two car doors slam, but I didn't turn around, not even when they drove off with a friendly honk.

How could I have done that to Cheyenne? It was like I'd lost every bit of horse sense I'd ever had. What was wrong with me?

Travis and I didn't have any trouble keeping up with Cheyenne. She stopped to graze, letting us just so close and no closer. Then she trotted away and did the same thing all over again.

"At least she's heading back toward Horse-feathers," Travis said.

After over an hour, Cheyenne crossed the road and wandered through an open gate. Finding herself fenced in on three sides, with us on the fourth, she stared at us and snorted. I reached down and picked a handful of grass, then held it out for her. On the third try I finally got close enough to grab her halter with one hand while she ate out of my other hand.

Travis slipped closer and pressed the lead rope into my palm. Slowly I snapped it onto the halter ring.

Cheyenne bolted at the tiny snapping sound, jerking away and pulling the rope through my fingers. My hand stung, but I held onto the end of the rope as she pulled backwards.

"Let her go, Scoop!" Travis cried.

But when Cheyenne couldn't get away, she finally gave in.

Cheyenne let me lead her out to the road and back toward Horsefeathers. Sheriff Orville was waiting for us by the side of the road. He followed us in the patrol car for about a half-mile until we waved him on. The horse shied at everything, scared even of the wind.

When we got to Horsefeathers, everybody had gone home. As soon as I turned Cheyenne loose, she tore to the back of the pasture, not even stopping to greet Moby and Orphan.

"What a night, huh?" Travis said as we climbed into his old white pick-up. "A Halloween to remember."

I'd remember it. I knew that. I glanced back at Horsefeathers, the paddock light shedding light on the scene of the crime, where black baled ashes looked like nothing more than shadows. The pain in my head had all slid to a spot right behind my eyeballs. "Travis," I whispered, "I almost lost everything."

He was quiet for a minute. "I know." He reached over and squeezed my arm. "You're shivering, Scoop," he said. He wriggled out of his jacket and pushed it at me.

But it wasn't the night chill that had me shaking. My mind wouldn't shut off the *what if's*. What if Horsefeathers really did catch fire? The firefighter said all it needed was six inches or a degree of wind. What if the wind had shifted directions? What if Orphan had been inside the barn? And what about Cheyenne? What if Cheyenne stayed wild? What if—?

"Scoop?" Travis was leaning over, his mouth inches from mine. The truck was stopped. "Want me to walk you in?"

I glanced up. We were in my driveway.

I thanked Travis and dragged myself inside to report to Dotty and B.C. That night I lay in bed, staring up at the ceiling of my attic room, where the roof peaks like the top of an "A." My head pounded, and I could almost hear my blood racing around in my veins and vessels.

I said my prayers and tried to be thankful that everything had turned out okay. Orphan and Horsefeathers were fine. Cheyenne was back. All the horses were safe.

But nothing felt fine or safe. It felt like I'd opened some door and glimpsed all the horrible possibilities on the other side. The fumes of fear were leaking into my world, and I couldn't close that door to shut them out.

For the next three weeks, we tried to find out who set fire to the hay bales. Maggie was convinced Stephen Dalton of Dalton Stables had done it. The sheriff thought it was a Halloween trick that got out of hand. Travis said we'd probably never know. Somehow that answer scared me most—that disaster could strike from anywhere it pleased and not get caught.

I worked with Cheyenne every day after school. Jen helped whenever she could, but she was still getting over being sick. Winter came early. It showed up almost overnight, shoving autumn out and blowing brown leaves from the trees.

"How's Cheyenne coming?" Maggie asked, as I was finishing up a tough workout one chilly afternoon. Steam rose from Cheyenne's sweaty neck. My hands were stiff from the cold.

When I turned to answer Maggie, Cheyenne used it as an excuse to throw a fit. She bucked once and tried to rear, but I pulled her out of it.

"I don't know what I'm doing wrong,

Maggie," I said, dismounting carefully. "Cheyenne has been afraid of everything since Halloween."

Moby and Orphan ambled over to get sugar lumps from Maggie. "That's weird," Maggie said, making Moby nod up and down to get her treat. They were both performers. "It's never taken you this long to bring Cheyenne around before, has it?"

"What are you saying, Maggie?" I snapped. Did she think *she* could do any better?

Maggie blinked her big brown eyes at me. Her coat, hat, and gloves were as red as her queen costume had been on Halloween night. Long, wavy hair flowed to her shoulders, mixed in with tiny braids and red ribbons. Even in the cold, she looked warm and ready to step onto the stage. "Whoa, Scoop," she said in her best pretend Southern accent. "I didn't mean a little ol' thing."

"Sorry, Maggie," I said, unsaddling Cheyenne. What hurt was that Maggie was right. It had never taken me so long to get through to Cheyenne, or to any other horse, for that matter. Cheyenne wasn't the only one who hadn't been the same since the Halloween fire. I'd changed too. "I don't know what's wrong," I said, hoisting the saddle down. "Sometimes I don't think I'll ever get Cheyenne to trust me again." Or *me* to trust me again, I thought.

Maggie took the saddle from me so I could cool off Cheyenne. "Do you think we'll ever know who set the Halloween fire?" she asked, shifting the saddle in her arms. "Let me rephrase that. Do you think we'll ever *prove* who did it? You know it had to be Stephen Dalton, no matter what he says."

"I don't know, Maggie," I said. Stephen's dad runs the biggest stable in our part of the state. You wouldn't think our little home for "backyard horses" would worry them, but it seems to. Still, as rotten as Stephen had always been to me, I couldn't believe he'd try to burn down Horsefeathers.

Maggie threw her head back and stared up at the gray sky. "Isn't it glorious!" she said dramatically. "I love winter!" She was obviously trying to change the subject, and I was glad to let her.

Maggie headed toward the barn, hugging Cheyenne's saddle. "All we need around here is a good, long break—lots of snow days and missed school!"

On the Tuesday before Thanksgiving, it looked as if Maggie might get her wish. The sky swirled with gray, puffy clouds that looked bottom heavy. Even inside school, it smelled like snow.

"Come on, snow!" Maggie whispered, squirming in homeroom, sitting between me and Carla. "Channel 7 News almost promised a blizzard!" Maggie was probably calling herself Maggie 37 Green today. She was pure green, from her pale green sweater to her army green pants and green plaid socks. And her accent had transformed to rolling R's and a Scottish brogue.

Poor Ms. Bowers, our freshman homeroom teacher, was trying everything to get us even half as excited as she was about writing our speeches on citizenship for the American Legion contest. "And don't forget," she said in a cheerleading voice, "three winners go on to district!"

Just about every guy in West Salem High School had a crush on Ms. Jo Bowers. For one thing, she was petite and had huge brown eyes and long, bouncy hair. Everything about her was bouncy. She's the only person I've ever called *perky*. It wore me out just watching her.

I'm never any good at speaking in class, much less giving a speech in front of a bunch of soldiers. But what I'd come to think of as Cheyenne's and my Halloween fear made the idea of giving a speech even more terrifying. What if I froze on stage? What if everybody squirmed in their seats while I tried to remember my lines? What if they laughed out loud at me?

"Is it possible that nobody has even one idea for a good speech?" Ms. Bowers looked poised to spring into a cheer for one good idea. But our brains had already checked out for Thanksgiving vacation, even though our bodies had to show up for another day.

That day just happened to be my birthday—not that anybody had remembered. Any other year, I might have reminded Jen or Maggie. I probably would have asked Carla and Ray and everybody to come over or to do something on my birthday. But not this time.

Every time I thought about saying something about my birthday to one of my friends, I thought of a dozen reasons why I shouldn't. What if they already knew it was my birthday? What if they thought it was dumb? What if they didn't care? What if I asked them and they didn't want to come?

Maggie's mother had the right idea. When Maggie was born, her mom gave her the middle name "37." Maggie claims it's her mother's lucky number, but it's also Maggie's birthday: March 7. 3–7. Everybody always knows when Maggie 37's birthday rolls around. Maybe I should have been named Sarah 11-23 Coop.

"Jen?" Good move by Ms. Bowers. Jen Zucker is the smartest kid in our class. She probably had her speech all planned out and half written.

"Yes," Jen said. "I would say it is entirely possible that nobody has even one idea for a good speech." Jen's blond hair fell in little wisps around her face. Maggie says Jen is "fine-boned," like ballerinas. Her gold, wire-rimmed glasses make her look smart, but pretty too. Jen may look like a fine-boned Arabian, but her temperament is more like a mustang—able, strong, and fiercely independent.

Petite Ms. Bowers looked like someone had stolen her pom-poms. If she'd been a horse, she might have been a miniature horse, everybody's favorite pet.

"Actually," Jen said, probably unwilling to dampen our teacher's spirits, "I do have a good idea, but I'm having trouble getting my hands on the reference book I need." Jen turned around and glared at Stephen Dalton. "*Somebody* is six weeks overdue on the library book I need for my speech."

"Don't have a cow," Stephen said, running his fingers through his greasy red hair. Even in this freezing weather, Stephen wore a thin, silky shirt and crisp pants with no wrinkles. "I've got that stupid book at home somewhere."

"A lot of good it does me there," Jen said.

Ms. Bowers groaned, and a few of the kids chuckled, the ones who weren't staring out at the darkening sky.

Screech! The PA intercom system squawked again: *Squawk!* "Will Sarah Coop please come to the office?" said the disembodied voice of the school secretary.

"Me?" Sarah Coop is my real name, but

everybody calls me Scoop. Almost everybody. For a minute, my mind flashed back to months before when the principal used to call me to the office to go look for my grandfather. He had Alzheimer's disease and used to wander off. Dotty would make them get me out of school to go find him. But Grandad had died in early fall.

"Oooh, Sarah," Stephen said, "what did you do this time?" Half a dozen kids turned all the way around in their chairs to stare at me. My throat went dry, and my face burned. Jen Zucker glanced back, her blue eyes narrowed. Everybody waited.

I stood up, knocking my books into the aisle.

Ray, one of my oldest buddies, picked them up and handed them to me. "Take it easy," he said. If he were a horse, he'd be a Tennessee Walker. Nothing ever upsets him.

I took the books, then set them on my desk, glancing up at the teacher and trying to imagine what I'd done to get called to the office.

Then I thought of B.C. What if something had happened to my brother? B.C. is what they call manic depressive. He gets in moods where he can do some pretty crazy things sometimes. What if—?

"Sarah Coop! Now! Come here right—" The voice over the intercom yelled. Then a woman's scream filled the room and echoed down the halls.

"Help! It's coming after me! Get it!"

"I think you better go—fast!" Ms. Bowers cried. "Skip your hall pass and run!"

My heart pounded so hard I couldn't catch my breath as I raced down the empty hall toward the office—toward the screams. Four or five teachers stuck their heads out of classrooms, but stayed safely on the other side of their doorways.

I kept my head down and tried to look invisible. What if B.C. had gone off the deep end? What if he'd taken the secretary hostage or spray painted the principal? Or, what if he—

Then I heard it—*clip, clop, clip, clop*. I zoomed around the corner and couldn't believe my eyes. Orphan, *my* horse, was strolling down the main hall of West Salem High School.

I blinked, but when I opened my eyes, Orphan was still standing in the hall outside the principal's office. Her black coat was caked with dirt, and her tail switched back and forth.

"Orphan?" I called.

She whinnied, then started down the hall toward me. Her back leg slipped on the concrete, then her forelegs, like Bambi on ice.

"Stay!" I yelled.

I ran to my horse. Something had to be terribly wrong for her to come to school.

Ms. Dorr appeared in the doorway of the principal's office. Instead of yelling at me, she sighed. "You're excused," she said. "So is your horse."

"Sorry," I said.

I hurried out of there, but slowed down when Orphan slipped again. Right in front of the boys' restroom, Orphan stopped and dropped a load of manure.

"Oooh, yuk!" said a couple of students across the hall. Miss Gilbert's language arts class huddled at the door and groaned.

Mr. Wilson, our janitor, shouted, "I'm not cleaning that! Not in my job description."

"I'm sorry, Mr. Wilson," I said. I didn't know what else to do, so I led Orphan out of the building. The second I stepped outside, I wished I'd thought to grab my coat. The wind whipped straight through me, and the air felt wet.

"What is it, girl?" I asked. I knew this wasn't a social call. Orphan wouldn't have wanted to venture inside that school any more than Ms. Dorr wanted her to.

Orphan bobbed her head up and down, up and down. She stamped with her foreleg, pounding the frozen ground. I shivered. I'd worn a sweatshirt over my T-shirt, but it didn't help. Still, as cold as I was, I wasn't about to go back into my classroom to get my coat.

Orphan didn't have her halter on, but I swung myself up on her back and told her to take me wherever she wanted. I buried my hands in her shaggy, black winter fur and leaned onto her neck to steal her warmth. My breath puffed to meet the steam that rose from her neck.

Orphan took off so fast I had to grip tighter with my knees and grab a handful of mane to stay on. She headed for Horsefeathers.

Please, God, I prayed, ***don't let it be another fire***.

The wind picked up, and the temperature kept dropping. When we turned into Horsefeathers Lane, I spotted Cheyenne. She was standing in front of the barn, tangled in a mess of ropes and strings that trailed from her hind legs. She must have gotten spooked in the barn, bolted through her stall, and pulled down the hay nets as she tore through the barn.

Orphan whinnied as we came up on the Paint. Cheyenne stood maybe 10 horse lengths away from us. I let Orphan walk all the way up to her and stop before I slid off.

"Hey, Chey," I said softly. "Nice of you to get me out of class, but I'm freezing. Let's go inside the barn, huh?"

Her muscles quivered. She arched her neck and snorted as I inched closer. Suddenly, when I was about three feet away from her, a picture of Halloween night flashed through my mind. I could see Cheyenne rearing, me falling.

I stopped. The wind reached through my sweatshirt like ice fingers. Sleet pelted my face, hit my shoulders, and bounced off. I pulled my sleeves down and let them act like mittens for my frozen hands.

Orphan nickered softly behind me. But I was afraid to reach for Cheyenne. What if she took off like the last time? With all that junk tangled around her legs she could really hurt herself. What if she reared up again and fell over backwards? I've seen it happen to horses more often than I like to admit.

We stood there in the sleet, getting iced over like everything else outside. Each *what if?* scenario seemed as real to me as the scene in front of me—Cheyenne standing tense, but still.

Finally, Orphan stepped past me, all the way up to Cheyenne. They nuzzled each other, then blew into one another's nostrils. I reached up and took hold of Cheyenne's halter.

She followed Orphan into the barn with a soldier's stride, on long, stiff legs. Soft nickers greeted us from all sides as I put Cheyenne back in her stall. I scooped an armful of hay into her feed trough. She nibbled on the hay while I loosed the strings from her hooves.

Angel, Travis' Appaloosa, stuck his head over the stall partition. Since Travis and Jen are brother and sister, that, in a way, makes Angel and Cheyenne brother and sister. I fed them, then grained Ham. And I felt foolish—grateful that nobody but Orphan had seen me shut down like that.

By the time I'd finished brushing Orphan, Moby had strolled in for her supper. I fed her the special "senior feed" Jen mixes just for her.

The wind was howling so fierce, I didn't know a car had driven up until I heard the door slam. Maggie 37 came running into the barn. "Is everything okay?" she asked dramatically. "Why did Orphan come to school? It's all anybody's talking about!"

Jen and Travis ducked into the barn, pushing the door shut after them.

"It's really something out there!" Travis shouted above the wind. His blond hair glistened with sleet and snow.

"Was it Cheyenne?" Jen asked. "As soon as I heard Orphan actually came to school, I knew Cheyenne had to be the reason."

"You guessed it," I said. "She'd pulled down hay nets and broken out of the barn."

"But you caught her okay?" Jen asked.

"Cheyenne's okay now. I just wish I could get her to trust me again." I should have said something about how Orphan had been the one to catch her, about how I'd frozen up again. Instead, I kept brushing Moby and tried not to let them see how scared I'd been.

"I hear Orphan left a souvenir," Travis said, the slight smile pulling at his big blue eyes. He looked at me, and his smile dissolved. "Scoop, where's your coat? You have to be freezing."

"I'm ok-kay," I said, but the *k* stuck in the middle of my chattering teeth.

"Maggie," Jen said, "didn't you get Scoop's coat?"

"I almost forgot," Maggie said. "It's in the truck. Want me to go get it?"

Travis unzipped his jacket, shrugged it off and put it over my shoulders. "Leave it," he said when I tried to give it back. "You can get yours later."

The coat felt warm with leftover Travis heat. I couldn't help inhaling the leather smell made better by having been close to him.

Maggie winked at me.

"Thanks, Travis," I said, a flash of warmth going through me.

"I will be *so* disappointed if we don't get our blizzard!" said Maggie, taking the brush from me and working on Moby. "I need a break. I don't want to do a thing except sleep late and watch cartoons and talk on the phone with everyone I know and say how wonderful it is to do absolutely nothing." She seemed to visualize her idyllic scene for all of two seconds. Then she changed her mind. "What am I saying? I'd be bored to death!"

Now! I told myself. This would be the perfect time to invite them to come over on my birthday. Maggie already said she wasn't doing anything. She said she'd be bored.

But what if Maggie said no? Or what if she said yes, but I could tell she'd rather say no? My house isn't exactly the most fun place to spend Thanksgiving vacation. Yeah, it would definitely be worse if she said yes, forced into it because she'd just admitted not having anything else to do.

Jen had joined Cheyenne in her stall, and Travis watched them intently from outside. I wondered what it would be like to have a family like that, where a big brother worried about his sister—not like I worry about B.C., because something's really wrong with him and you can't help but worry about him. But worry like Travis seems to, when there's really no need.

"Well, Miss Maggie 37," Jen said, "*you* may get a break at Thanksgiving, but I certainly do not." She stroked her horse and finger-combed Cheyenne's mane. "Thanksgiving dinner is no picnic at the Zucker household. Right, Travis? Besides the 11 of us, there will be Granny and Gramps Zucker and Grandma and Grandpa Aimes. We're cooking two turkeys. And I have to peel a million potatoes and slice a million apples for pies, not to mention the pumpkins."

That cinched it. No way was I inviting Jen to come over, not with all those apples and potatoes waiting. On the other hand, maybe she'd like the chance to get away from all that work for a while.

"You're so lucky, Jen!" Maggie said, going for a French accent. "At least you will not be how-you-say? *bored.*"

I took a deep breath and let it out. "You know," I said, not looking at them, straightening and re-straightening Orphan's forelock, "you guys could come to my house tomorrow."

Their silence filled the barn.

"I mean, if we get snowed out of school? Or even after school? Well, tomorrow is my birthday—no big deal or anything. We could just hang out or whatever." I laughed nervously, wishing somebody would say something. Anything. "Build snowmen? Make snow angels?"

Stop talking. Don't say another word. You're making it worse. Keep your stupid mouth shut.

Still, nobody spoke—not Maggie, not Jen, not Travis. Orphan sneezed, and I was thankful for the distraction.

I glanced in Maggie's direction. Out of the corner of my eye, I caught her gesturing to Jen, lifting her shoulders. A *what-should-I-say?* gesture. Jen grimaced and raised her eyebrows.

Travis shrugged. Even *he* was in on it— whatever *it* was. *It* was probably another plan, a plan that didn't include me or my birthday.

"Hey, no big thing," I said. I should have listened to my *what-if* instinct and just kept my mouth shut.

6

W ednesday—tomorrow—isn't a good day for Travis and me," Jen said awkwardly. "We ... we already have plans."

"Me too," Maggie said softly.

They had plans? *I* had a birthday, and I didn't have plans. "No, I understand. You've got to get a jump on those potatoes," I said, trying to make out like it didn't hurt, like my throat didn't burn with a sadness I couldn't explain.

"I *do* need to ride over to Stephen Dalton's house and get that library book if we don't have school," Jen said. "Would you have time to ride over with me, Scoop? Say ... afternoon, two?"

I shrugged. "Sure." I picked up Orphan's left foreleg, pretended to examine her hoof, then set it back down.

"I have to go to a Chesley family reunion on Thursday for Thanksgiving, to Kennsington," Maggie said. "It's at my stepdad's parents. They're okay, but I'm the only kid who's not like a little brat. There'll be like a dozen kids younger than my stepbrothers, and everybody expects me to keep an eye on the little kids. And they throw food at each other! It's disgusting!"

I tried to laugh.

"You know what?" Travis said, shooting little glances at me that made me want to cry. I couldn't stand being pitied. That felt a hundred times worse than the fact that they obviously had *plans* that didn't include my birthday.

"What, Travis?" Maggie asked.

"If you really don't want to go to your stepdad's relatives for Thanksgiving, maybe you could go to Scoop's on Thursday." Travis sounded so hopeful, I almost felt sorry for him.

"Travis," I said, "don't be silly. Maggie wants to go to Kennsington. She's just being dramatic."

"No, listen," Maggie said, as if warming to the idea. "That's a great idea! And I'm not kidding either. I don't want to go to the Chesley's. My mother wouldn't make me either, not if I had something else to do. She knows what it's like for me there. Even my stepfather wouldn't really care."

I said, "You—you mean you'd like to come to my house—for Thanksgiving? It's just Dotty and B.C. and me. Nothing fancy." I tried to keep my voice light and not let on how much I wanted Maggie to come. Thanksgivings had always been a little sad. Family holiday things made me miss my folks. It had been almost eight years since they'd died in an explosion at the bottle plant. But holidays had a way of making me feel like my parents had just died and this was the first celebration without them.

"Really, Scoop," Maggie said, "it would be the perfect solution! Would Dotty mind, do you think?"

"I'm sure she wouldn't," I said. "It's the one meal she actually uses the oven for. Let's go tell her right now. I told her I'd stop by Hy-Klas after school anyway."

I could hardly wait to see Dotty's face when she found out Maggie would be with us. B.C. would go ballistic. He thinks Maggie hung the moon. I didn't care what everybody was doing without me on Wednesday. Thursday, Maggie and I could spend the whole day together. I was already starting to feel Thanksgiving.

Travis dropped us off at the Hy-Klas grocery store, where Dotty had worked since she took on B.C. and me the day after our folks were killed.

Dotty had shown up the day before the funeral with one battered suitcase and a brown sack with a store-bought angel food cake in it. The day after the funeral, Dotty walked into the Hy-Klas and started straightening shelves. Mr. Ford hired her on the spot. I'd never seen Cinnamon Lake, the town about two hours south where Dotty'd lived in her own apartment. And as far as I knew, she'd never gone back.

"Scoop," Jen called as Maggie and I climbed out of the back seat, "don't forget. If we don't have school, we'll ride over to Dalton's in the afternoon. Cheyenne could use the workout. Plus, it's the only way I'll ever get that book from Stephen."

Maggie and I waved as Travis' white pickup coughed its way down Main Street. The heater in the truck hadn't worked, so I was back to being frozen. My own coat was about half as warm as Travis' coat. Plus, it didn't smell like his.

Sleet mixed with snow came down harder. Bare tree branches looked like glass as ice formed around them. Behind us a limb cracked like the snap of a whip. Maggie and I clung to each other, slipping on the sidewalk up to the store.

Inside the store, Maggie and I shifted our feet and blew into our hands to get the feeling back. "I'm starving!" Maggie said.

"You came to the right place, Ms. 37," I said, pointing to shelves of candy and chips.

"I didn't bring my purse," Maggie whined.

"Get what you want. Dotty can pay, and we'll pay her back. Get me a candy bar too."

But Dotty wasn't at her usual post, first register in check-out. I spotted her in the central office, a raised platform squared off with glass panels. I headed over. Mr. Ford seemed to be lecturing my aunt and the new check-out girl, Gail Gayle, Mr. Ford's niece.

Standing side-by-side, Gail and my aunt Dotty looked about as opposite as two people can. Gail is model tall and skinny. Dotty barely comes up to Gail's chin, and she refuses to set foot on scales, being what Maggie calls pleasingly plump. Gail's hair was sleek and shiny, cut short in sharp angles. About half of it was dyed in a weird shade of red-purple. Dotty's hair always looks the same, coarse and brown. It hung carelessly to the base of her neck. Her straight bangs were too chunky and too long, reaching her thick brown glasses so her nose looked framed. Where Dotty wore only a small gold cross around her neck, Gail Gayle wore four silver necklaces. She sported rings on all her fingers, one ring in her nose, and about seven or eight rings lining each ear like silver rivets on a harness. The orange apron that hung loose on Gail, bulged and strained around my aunt.

I moved closer to them in case Dotty could break away for a minute. I couldn't wait to tell her that Maggie wanted to come to our house for Thanksgiving.

Dotty lifted her chin in a wave, but quickly turned back to Mr. Ford, whose lips kept moving fast, although the rest of his face looked set in stone.

Gail had a smirk on her face that didn't change when I smiled and nodded at her. She snapped her gum and sighed.

Hoping Mr. Ford's lecture wouldn't be too bad or too long, I eased closer.

"And another thing," Mr. Ford was saying, glaring straight at Dotty, "shoplifting is up—*way* up."

Dotty gasped. "I just can't imagine it!" she cried. If Dotty were a horse, at first you'd think she was an ordinary pony, but she's really more like a Cob, strong and dependable. I knew for a fact that she did half of Gail's work without complaining. None of this was her fault. I bit my lip so hard I tasted blood.

"And that's exactly the problem, Dotty," he said. "You *have* to imagine it. People are taking advantage of you. And they're taking *my* goods right from under your nose!"

I couldn't stand hearing Mr. Ford talk to Dotty like that. She was the best worker anybody ever had, and he wasn't being fair.

"But who would shoplift, Mr. Ford?" Dotty shook her head.

As if on cue, Maggie strolled up the aisle toward me and shouted, "Hey Scoop! Catch! Milky Way okay?" She zinged a candy bar at me. I missed, and the candy thumped against Mr. Ford's office window.

He stepped down out of his office with Dotty behind him. He leaned over, picked up the Milky Way, and held it out to me. "Is this yours?" he asked, his eyes tiny as yellow bot fly eggs.

I broke out in a cold sweat and couldn't speak. I knew what he was thinking. When I was 10, I did shoplift. My parents had been dead for three years, but that summer, for some reason, it felt like they'd just died. I'd taken gum, never anything else, and I never chewed it. The next day I'd put it back. That was when Mr. Ford had caught me—putting back the gum and straightening the rows. Dotty had explained God's forgiveness to me that very day. I'd believed the forgiveness Christ offered me, and I'd never even thought about shoplifting again.

But I knew Mr. Ford hadn't forgotten or forgiven.

"What's up?" asked Maggie 37, her mouth full of chips that smelled like Bar-B-Q. "Is it okay? Can I come for Thanksgiving?"

"Thanksgiving? Why, gracious goodness yes!" Dotty exclaimed, pushing past Mr. Ford to give Maggie a hug. "Now ain't that the best news! Maggie coming to give thanks with us. Won't B.C. be surprised!"

Mr. Ford cleared his throat. "Dotty, I'm sorry. I'm going to need you to work for me Thanksgiving."

He had to be kidding. Nobody worked on Thanksgiving.

"I'm so short on profits this month," he explained. "I have to make it up. And we'll be the only store still open for people who forgot their sweet potatoes or pumpkin pies. I've placed ads in three papers. My supply man in Kennsington said he has a store there that saw its biggest profits on holidays."

"That's not fair!" I said it so loud, even Gail stopped chewing her gum.

Mr. Ford's mouth pressed to a straight line, and his tiny, beebee eyes narrowed at me, accusing me.

"Why can't Gail work Thanksgiving?" I pleaded. "You don't need two checkers."

"We're having a big family dinner. I can't work," Gail said.

Right. Gail was the boss' niece. Dotty was nobody. All I wanted was my aunt and my friend to spend Thanksgiving with me. Was that too much to ask?

I felt Maggie's hand on my shoulder. "It's okay, Scoop. Maybe next year. The Chesley's won't be so bad."

Dotty came over and hugged me. "Thanksgiving is the Lord's day, Scoop," she said. "We can be thankful no matter where we're at."

Her hug made her nametag dig into my chest, the nametag Mr. Ford made her wear. It said, *Hi! I'm Dottie!*—spelled wrong, with an "ie" where a "y" should have been. Dotty wore it every single day, as if anybody who walked in off the street had a right to call her by her first name, but she better not call them by theirs.

Dottie, like it didn't even matter how you spelled it because *she* didn't really matter.

"No!" I said. "It's not right, Dotty!"

Mr. Ford glared at me, then glanced at his watch. But I didn't care.

"Can't you even give her a nametag with her name spelled right?" I asked.

"What?" he said, only half listening.

"It's *Dotty*—D-o-t-t-y. She deserves for you to spell her name right!" I couldn't stop myself. It was like my Halloween fear had suddenly shifted to anger, pouring out as fast as a bucketful of *what if's.* I couldn't control the anger any more than I could the fear. "And she deserves to get Thanksgiving off too! Just because *we* won't be sitting in some fancy dining room like you and Gail here and—"

"Scoop!" Dotty said, her voice a squeak, like shoes on the gym floor. She put her hand on my arm, but I couldn't stop.

"Dotty deserves this holiday off, and you're going to give it to her!"

Mr. Ford's thin lips folded in and disappeared. He closed his eyes, then opened them slowly. "You're right," he said. "Your aunt deserves better."

Yes! I did it! Finally, I'd actually done something right. I'd stood up for Dotty. I'd let my anger override my fears. I'd made her boss see how valuable she was.

"Dotty," Mr. Ford said, almost tenderly. "You've been much too important around here for me to go on like this. I guess I was hoping to put this off until after the holidays. But that would be selfish of me. It's better to tell you now." His thin chest heaved. He wiped one hand down his face. "Dotty, I'm going to have to let you go."

Maggie gasped.

A cold shiver started in my toes and traveled like lightning to the top of my head.

Dotty squinted up at Mr. Ford. "Let me go," she repeated. "I'm fired?" She asked it in a voice I'd never heard before, the way she might have sounded when she was a little girl. She turned and stared at me as if she couldn't remember who I was. "I'm ... fired."

7

Mr. Ford's face wrinkled from his forehead to his narrow chin. "Dotty, believe me, this is as hard on me as it is on you. You've been a good worker. But that superstore in Hamilton is drawing off my customers." He glanced at Gail. "Margaret—I mean, Mrs. Ford thinks Gail needs to stay here and work. Otherwise, I'd keep you on."

"I'm fired," Dotty repeated, still looking stunned. Her glassy-eyed stare was enough to melt my anger right back into fear. What was she going to do without the Hy-Klas?

"Dotty?" I said. "I'm so sorry." I turned to Mr. Ford, wiping away tears with the back of my hand. "Please? Maggie and I were going to pay for that food. We don't shoplift."

"Of course you don't!" Dotty exclaimed. "Nobody was accusing you girls of nothing. Ain't that right, Mr. Ford?"

Mr. Ford's lips twitched. His eyebrows arched, then flattened.

"Scoop would never steal!" Dotty sounded

as angry as I'd ever heard her. Her face reddened. "You—don't tell me you really think—why she ain't—" Dotty closed her eyes. "Lord Jesus, help me," she said.

And He did. You could see it when she opened her eyes. She straightened her nametag and glanced at her checkout counter. "Scoop, you go home and see to B.C., will you, Hon? I gotta stay to closing." She made her way to the front of the store to wait on a customer at her register.

Maggie led me out of the Hy-Klas in a daze. The wind blew so hard she had to shoulder the door open. Color had drained from the world. Snow lay like a blanket, with bumps for cars and curbs, buildings and trees.

"You better come to my house," Maggie shouted over the wind. Maggie's house was only a block away. "You don't want to walk home in this."

I shook my head. "B.C.'s home alone," I said, pulling my jacket around me tighter and stuffing my hands into the pockets. "I'll be okay."

But I didn't feel okay—and it wasn't just the snow. I had gotten Dotty fired. Now what were we going to do?

It took me over twice as long as usual to get home. Scarves of snow whipped under street lights and swirled in open spaces. Snow fell harder, blinding me when I tried to look up. Fear clung to me like snow to branches, changing the look of everything.

By the time I turned up our drive, I was a walking snowman.

"B.C.!" I hollered from the porch, stomping some of the snow off.

There was no answer from the house.

"B.C.!" Panic choked off my call. He should have been there. Why wouldn't he answer? I walked through the house, clicking on lights. The downstairs felt chilled and smelled like onions and rotten potatoes. "B.C.!" I hollered upstairs.

A light streamed out from under B.C.'s door, the tiny room off the living room. It used to be Grandad's bedroom. I knocked on the door. "B.C.?" I asked softly, trying to keep the panic out of my voice. I pushed the door open, expecting a hundred horrible things on the other side.

B.C. sat cross-legged in the middle of a bottle cap fort. Metal caps, three or four caps high, encircled my brother. Our dad used to come home every evening after his day shift at the bottle plant and bring B.C. a pocketful of bottle caps. I don't even remember when we started calling my brother "B.C.," for "Bottle Cap." He was only 2 years old when Dad was killed. Our mom was killed too. If she had been on her night shift, she would have been safe, but she'd gone in early so she could see Dad before she started work.

For a year afterward, B.C. waited every night by the door, as if Dad would surprise everybody by walking in with a pocketful of bottle caps.

B.C. looked small and thin and out of proportion in the middle of those bottle caps. His bushy brown hair reminded me of a squirrel's tail. His head seemed too big for his little body, which was wrapped around itself in a tight ball, rocking back and forth.

"What's up, B.C.?" I asked, swallowing my fear, trying to pray.

He looked up at me, his eyes red, his cheeks wet. "Where—were—you?" he asked between sobs.

"I was—" but I knew he didn't really want to know where I'd been, what I'd been through. I should have been home for him. "What's wrong, B.C.?" I sat on his bed, with B.C. on the floor at my feet. Before the room was B.C.'s or Grandad's, it had been a laundry room. B.C.'s little bed barely fit along the longest wall, with one dresser and a tiny wastebasket taking up the other.

"A huge blizzard is coming here!" B.C. screamed. "Tommy Zucker said it could get higher than our house and nobody could get in or out! And I thought you and Dotty would get snowed out and I'd be snowed in." Tears flowed down his cheeks.

I felt horrible. First I'd hurt Dotty. And now B.C. "I'm sorry, B.C." How many things could I keep being sorry for? I tried to pat his head, but he pulled away.

"You're always sorry! But I was scared! I was really, really scared, and you weren't here!"

"You're not the only one who's scared, B.C.," I said, letting my guard down.

B.C. looked as shocked as if I'd turned into a giant bottle cap. "Who else is scared?"

The door of fear inside me cracked open wider, and I saw more of the terrors on the other side. We'd been living from paycheck to paycheck, barely scraping by. And now we wouldn't have Dotty's Hy-Klas paycheck. I was barely making payments at Horsefeathers, and winter was the roughest time because I had to buy hay and more grain. Now what would we do?

"*I'm* scared," I said, hoping that would help B.C. realize he wasn't alone. He wasn't the only one fighting fear.

"You are?" he asked, sitting up straight. Through the window, snow-reflected moonlight streamed in and lit half of B.C.'s face. For a second he looked so much like our dad I ached. I'd been adopted. Then they'd had B.C. regular. I wondered if he'd keep looking more and more like them.

"Are you really scared, Scoop?" B.C. asked, amazed. At least for the moment, the thought of his big sis being scared seemed to take his mind off his own fears. "Are you afraid of the storm too?"

"Not of the storm," I said. "I don't like getting so cold, but I love the snow. And if it snows a lot, we could get out of school. You'd like that, B.C."

"That would be cool," B.C. said. "I hate school." He picked up a handful of bottle caps and let them drop through his fingers and clatter onto the floor. "So why *are* you afraid, Scoop?"

I could smell stale pickle juice coming from under B.C.'s bed. "I guess I'm mostly afraid where we'll get the money to pay bills—now that I got Dotty fired." The second it slid out of my mouth, I knew I'd made a mistake, a big mistake.

B.C. curled up and held his knees. His whole body started shaking. "Poor Dotty," he muttered. "Poor Dotty. Poor Dotty."

"B.C.?" I knelt down and reached across his bottle cap fort to touch his head. Sparks shot from his hair with a *pffft*, static electricity making his hair look alive. "It's going to be okay." Inside I prayed: *God, please help it be okay. I can't do anything right. Just stop me from doing anything else wrong.*

I tried to get B.C. to play checkers or get a snack or watch cartoons, but nothing did any good. He stayed inside his bottle cap fort. He'd probably built it from inside. He hadn't made a door or a window. I wanted to crawl inside of his fort with him and see if his bottle caps could keep out my own fears.

Instead I stayed on his bed and watched ice make spider patterns on the window as the snow piled up and drifted like sand in the corners of the panes.

Finally I heard Dotty's car gunning up the driveway. I met her at the door and took the white plastic bags she was carrying. She didn't look like a woman who'd just lost her job. Maybe Mr. Ford had changed his mind. Maybe Gail Gayle had quit and Dotty was rehired.

"What a wonderland!" Dotty declared, pulling off her snow-covered shoes. "I ain't seen snow this pretty for I-don't-know-how long! I seen a bare bush out yonder what looks like a giant cotton ball!"

I took her wet coat before she could throw it on the sofa. I wanted her to tell me it was all fixed. Mr. Ford had just been kidding. "So?" I asked, when I couldn't wait another second. "Did he hire you back?"

"What?" Dotty asked, looking completely baffled. "Mr. Ford?"

No. The Secretary of Defense, I wanted to say.

Dotty shook snow out of her hair. "No. But don't you worry none. God will provide. He always does." She tugged off her scarf. "That poor man liked to give hisself ulcers over that there store of his."

Dotty was already starting to feel sorry for her ex-boss! I could hear it in her voice.

"Where's B.C.?" she asked, shaking herself wet-dog-like. A bobby pin fell to the carpet and we left it there.

"He hasn't come out of his room," I said. "He's scared."

Dotty's forehead wrinkled. "Storm got to him?"

"That, and I accidentally told him you were fired," I admitted.

While Dotty coaxed and prayed B.C. out of his fort, I unpacked the groceries. Already I could see life would be different. No cold cuts or fruit salads in Styrofoam containers. Dotty had brought home the generic box pudding that you have to pour milk in and wait on. Everything else was in cans, like we were destined to be holed up inside B.C.'s fort for months, for years maybe.

The phone rang. "I'll get it!" I yelled.

"Hello?" I said, glancing out at the huge flakes piling up outside.

"Oh, hello. Uh—Scoop, this is Mr. Ford."

I jerked the phone away from my ear and stared at it, as if Mr. Ford himself might come out of the receiver.

"Scoop? Hello? Hello?" His voice sounded

muffled, as if he were trapped under a snowdrift.

It would serve him right. He'd fired Dotty. He thought I was a thief. What gave him the right to call us? This was still our house. And he didn't get to boss Dotty or me around any more.

Slowly, soundlessly, I slipped the telephone back. I hung up on Mr. Ford.

Seconds later it rang again, just half a ring. I lifted the receiver an inch and set it back down. Heart pounding, I kept staring at the phone. What would I say if he called back? Would I pretend it had been the storm?

But Mr. Ford didn't call back.

At the kitchen table, Dotty said grace like she meant it. We ate canned bean-and-ham soup with pork 'n' beans and leftover three-bean salad. Dotty chatted about the weather, but B.C. and I didn't say much.

I didn't tell her about Mr. Ford's phone call.

B.C. went straight to bed after supper. I took a bath and tried not to imagine how things would be from here on out.

I was on the stairs on my way up to bed when I heard Dotty's voice. She'd pulled the phone as far as it would reach away from B.C.'s room. I was afraid it might be Mr. Ford, telling her how I'd hung up on him, so I stopped and listened.

Dotty was using her one-of-the-gals voice, so I figured she was just talking to the Hat Lady.

B.C. had begun calling Dotty's friend "the Hat Lady" because she sits in front of us at church and wears big hats every Sunday.

"Well," Dotty was saying, "I'm sure the good Lord knows what He's doing. Thick-headed as I am, I reckon I'll be a while afore I see His plan though."

She listened, winding the phone cord around her finger. I knew I shouldn't eavesdrop, but I couldn't help myself.

"I reckon that's right. The manager back in Cinnamon Lake said I'd always have me a job back at her office. I ain't seen her in three years, but I gets a card at Christmas and my birthday regular as dawn."

A job back in Cinnamon Lake? I didn't know Dotty had worked in some woman's office. I just figured there must have been a Hy-Klas back there. I didn't remember any Christmas or birthday cards from Cinnamon Lake.

Dotty walked back through the living room, and I scurried on up the stairs out of sight.

Was Dotty considering moving back to Cinnamon Lake? What if that woman offered Dotty her old job back? What if she offered lots of money? Maybe Dotty missed her old town and her old friends.

I climbed into bed without telling Dotty good night. My room was so cold, there was as much frost inside the window as outside. Snuggling under the pile of quilts, I prayed. *God, I'm so scared. Please give Dotty a good job close to home. I don't want her to move back to Cinnamon Lake.*

Then, without my knowing when, my prayers slipped into *what if's*. And I fell asleep to a chorus: *What if Dotty can't find another job? What if she moves to Cinnamon Lake? What about B.C. and me and Horsefeathers and Orphan? What if ... what if ... what if?*

Wednesday morning I woke up to a blinding whiteness. Sunlight sparkled on the snow outside my window and sent a beam like a spotlight into my room. I jumped out of bed and ran to look outside. Pure white covered everything in our yard. November 23, my birthday. "Happy Birthday to me," I said under my breath. Shivering, I pulled on jeans and a sweatshirt and wooly socks. How could it be so cold when there was so much sunshine?

I stopped on the stairs to listen to the scratchy radio noise trickling up from the kitchen. Something about the country twang voice and the static carried excitement. We only listened to that station on days school might get cancelled.

B.C., still in cowboy pajamas Tommy Zucker would never be caught dead in, raced to the stairs and hollered up at me. "No school! No school! They're scared to let us go in the snow!"

"Cool!" I said, jumping the last three steps to the ground.

"I thought you were never going to wake up!" It didn't take a genius to see that B.C. had undergone a mood switch overnight. He shouted every word and moved his arms in wild gestures. "Dotty wouldn't let me wake you up! Happy Birthday, Scoop!" He grabbed my hand and dragged me to the kitchen.

Dotty joined B.C. for maybe the worst rendition ever sung of "Happy Birthday to You!"

Dotty hugged me, although B.C. still hadn't let go of my hand. "How's it feel being an old woman of 15?" she asked. "Lord, You are so faithful to have grown up this young woman before me. I thank You Jesus, that I seen it happen close-up with my own two eyes. Sorry we didn't get you a cake."

The last part was to me. "That's okay, Dotty," I said, trying not to think of how sad it was that a 15-year-old girl didn't even get a cake on her birthday, not to mention a party or a friend staying over.

"Well," Dotty went on, "in all the hubbub last night, I plumb forgot the cake up at the Hy-Klas."

B.C. kept pulling me. "Lookee what we did!" he yelled. "Light it, Dotty!"

In the middle of the kitchen table, set on the plastic green and white table cloth, was a single cinnamon roll, broken off of a rectangle of them. On top were a bunch of orange and black and green jelly beans.

"See?" B.C. shouted. "Get it? There's 15 jelly beans—like you're 15."

Dotty struck a match and lit the single pink candle stuck in the middle of the roll.

B.C. shoved a lump of wrinkled newspapers at me. "I wrapped it myself!" he exclaimed.

There was definitely something inside the newspaper. I shook it. "Is it ... bottle caps?" I teased.

"No!" shouted B.C. "Open it!"

Dotty bit her bottom lip, looking as anxious as B.C.

I tore the paper back. Inside was a beautiful leather halter. I inhaled it, smelling cherries and tack rooms, and fine leather boots. "It's wonderful!" I said, something balling up in my throat. I'd never owned a leather halter. "Orphan will love it." It would have cost Dotty a day's wage, and now she didn't even get a wage. "But Dotty," I said, "we can't afford—"

"Now what kind of birthday talk is that?" she said. She turned her back and shuffled to the fridge, her shoes squeaking on the gray linoleum. "Better blow out that there candle. I ain't got much time."

"Are you going to the Hy-Klas?" I asked, wondering if Mr. Ford would squeal on me how I hung up on him. I blew out the candle on my cinnamon roll.

"No, I ain't," Dotty answered, closing the

fridge without getting anything out, still not looking at me.

I hadn't noticed before, but Dotty was dressed up. She had on her black church dress with a black bead necklace.

"Why are you dressed like that?" I asked, knowing that I should have told her she looked nice. But my stomach was getting that feeling like something was crawling inside of it, scratching to get out.

"Well," she said, tugging her skirt down over her stockings, which were the fake kind that are supposed to look like panty hose, but really only go to your knee. "I'm going to drive up to Cinnamon Lake, talk to a couple of folks I know there. My old boss up that way knows her a mess of people. She might know of something closer by—somebody needing an old ex-grocery worker." She faked a laugh, bending down to give her fake stockings another tug.

Cinnamon Lake? What if she'd already talked to her old boss and wasn't telling me everything? Maybe she'd gotten all gussied up because she *wanted* to move back there. "Are you sure the roads are safe?" I asked, surprised how regular my voice sounded, considering that I felt like screaming at her not to go. "Maybe ... maybe you shouldn't go, Dotty. I mean, in this storm and all."

"I got me an interview," she said, her face

letting go of some of the forehead wrinkles, like she was relieved I hadn't gone nuts on her. But I had. Just inside, where she couldn't see.

"I called that nice man from the highway patrol, and he said they've cleared off Route 89 already," Dotty reported. "They're expecting more snow, but I should get home before that hits. Will you young'uns be okay? Mercy, you ain't a young'un at all no longer. I'm right sorry to leave you on your birthday, Scoop." She was shoving herself into her old tweed coat. "Maybe you can get some of your friends over since you kids ain't got school? Make a snowman?"

"Good idea," I said, knowing it wasn't, knowing my friends all had *plans* that didn't include me. Even Dotty had *plans*. I was the only one on earth without plans—and it was *my* birthday.

B.C. and I followed Dotty to the door. Huge icicles hung from our roof. Each clear, rippled spear of ice slanted toward the driveway because of the constant winds.

"Drive carefully!" I yelled, as Dotty backed out of the driveway, plowing through a drift.

The crisp air felt so clean, I closed my eyes and inhaled. I didn't want to think about Dotty or her interview or Mr. Ford or the Hy-Klas or everybody's *plans*. It was *my* birthday, and it was up to me to enjoy it.

"B.C.," I said, breathing in air that froze my

nose hairs. "It's a beautiful day for a birthday! And I know exactly where I want to spend it."

I rushed to the closet, pulled on boots, gloves, my old winter jacket, and the knit hat that makes me look like a bank robber. "Get dressed and bundle up. You're coming with me to Horsefeathers!"

The snow was too dry to make snowballs, so B.C. and I threw handfuls of snow at each other all the way to the barn. He looked like a sleeping bag in the quilted snowsuit Dotty had gotten him at least two winters ago. Maybe by next winter it would fit him.

Orphan stood straight-legged in the middle of the paddock. When she saw us, she let out a long, tremoring whinny.

"Orphan!" I yelled.

She took off at a gallop, stopped short, then kicked her heels high. Moby ran after her, looking more like 4 years old than 24 years old. They pranced to the railing to meet me.

"Let's make angels," I whispered, like we were up to some huge secret. I climbed over the fence, and B.C. rolled under it, disappearing in the snow for an instant.

Orphan followed me, and Moby followed her, and B.C. followed Moby. Ham and Angel stepped out of the barn as if they were walking on water. Each step seemed to surprise them. Then Angel got brave. The Appaloosa trotted back and forth, snorting at the snow. Ham nodded up and down, then nuzzled the snow, eating and licking at the white fluff.

I stroked Orphan with my gloves. "Ready?" I asked her. Then I held my arms out to my side, closed my eyes, and let my body fall backward into the soft snow. It always reminds me of the "trust exercise" our first-grade teacher made us do. She'd tell us to close our eyes and let ourselves fall backward, trusting that she or another kid would catch us.

I lay in the snow a minute, brightness coming through my closed eyelids. I smelled hay and Orphan and winter.

A glass jar. That's what I needed! I wanted to gather the air of my fifteenth birthday and save it forever in a jar, just like Grandad used to do. He'd collected air from days filled with everything—from his wife's smile to the cries over Pearl Harbor. With a smooth, steady motion, I swung both arms toward my ears and pulled them back down. I did the same motion with my legs, out and in, out and in.

"I can make a snow angel too!" B.C. screamed beside me. He plopped next to me in the snow, and I heard him grunt as he moved his arms and legs.

"Down, Orphan!" I called. "Lie down. Roll!"

Several yards away Orphan's front legs buckled. She tipped forward. Then her back legs bent, and she was lying in the snow. She plopped over on her side, her legs sticking straight out toward me. I sat up to watch and saw Moby imitating Orphan a couple of feet over.

Orphan rolled onto her back and twisted back and forth in the snow, over and over again, as if giving herself a back scratch. I scrambled to my feet and looked at the angel I'd made in the snow. "Let's see yours, Orphan!" I shouted.

With a graceful flip, Orphan rolled all the way over and stepped to her feet, shaking off the snow. Moby rolled in the snow, then sprang up next to Orphan.

"Look, B.C.!" I shouted, running over to the horses. "Horsefeathers! Can't you see it?"

B.C. trudged over to me and stared at the dips and ripples left in the paddock snow, the perfect horse angels made by the rolling horses. "See what?" he asked.

"Horse angels! See?" To me, the patterns in the snow looked just like horses with wings.

"You're crazy, Scoop," B.C. said, studying the snow.

I whistled for the other horses. Cheyenne stayed just inside the barn, but the others came trotting over and joined in. Pretty soon we were all rolling in the snow, making birthday snow angels—all except Cheyenne.

"I wish Cheyenne would trust me enough to

come over and play with us," I said, brushing off snow that had worked up around my neck.

We played for a while longer, then B.C. helped with chores—mostly by keeping Dogless, our barn cat, out of my way. Dogless' home in the hayloft was twice as warm as my bedroom. He purred like electric horse clippers, no matter what B.C. did to him or how weird my brother held him.

Since it was my birthday, I dished out two helpings of everything. We hung up hay nets and filled them with hay in case we got another blizzard and the horses had to stay in the barn.

As soon as we left the barn, B.C. put on his brakes and grabbed my arm. "What's wrong with the sky?" he asked, his voice quivering.

"Nothing, B.C.," I said. But something had happened while we were brushing and cleaning stalls. That new blizzard Dotty had mentioned must have blown in at thoroughbred speed. Dark purple skies made it look like night outside. New snow fell fast, mixing with the blowing snow off the ground and more snow that flew off the barn roof. Everything got lost in a thick, white fog.

B.C.'s grip tightened on my arm. "I don't like it," he said. "I want to go home!"

By the time we got to the bottom of Horsefeathers Lane, snow was coming down so hard I couldn't look up without hurting my eyeballs.

B.C. hid his face in my jacket and clung to me, making it a hundred times harder to walk.

When we finally got home, it was almost two. I was so cold I took the hottest bath I could stand, sinking into the steamy water a little at a time. I had nothing better to do. No *plans*.

One good thing about our ancient bathroom is the big, deep bathtub. It's supposed to stand on four white feet, but several years back, Dotty slipped in the tub. She didn't break any bones, just one of the bathtub feet. We stacked two bricks under that side of the tub, and it looks kind of funny, but it works. The white part on the inside of the tub is chipped in chunks, down to something black that smells like rust. But when I fill that tub, I can float in it, and I think it's the best bathtub in the whole world.

B.C. camped out in the living room. I heard him dragging out all his bottle caps and turning on every light downstairs. I don't know how long I soaked in the tub. I had almost drifted off to sleep when I heard the phone ring. A minute later, B.C. banged on the bathroom door.

"Telephone! Scoop!" he yelled.

"You handle it, B.C!" I yelled back. "I'm taking a bath."

Bang, bang, bang, bang, bang! "They want you!"

"Tell them I'll call them back," I pleaded.

My skin felt warm and was just starting to wrinkle—warm for the first time in three days.

"They want you NOW!" B.C. screamed.

I slapped the surface of the water, splashing myself, water catching in one eye. *"Who* wants me now?"

"Tommy Zucker!" B.C. yelled back.

Tommy Zucker? He's the same age as B.C., and every bit as ornery—Jen's sneakiest brother by far. No way I was getting out of this bath so Tommy Zucker could say, "Cold enough for you?" or "You're all wet" and laugh like crazy.

"I'll call him when I get out!" I yelled. Then I held my breath and sank underwater.

When I surfaced, B.C. had left me alone. I soaked in the tub until the heat went out of the water and into me. Then I dried off, wrapped my hair in a towel and found B.C. He was behind the sofa, playing war—the good bottle caps (blue letters on the cap) versus the bad bottle caps (red-lettered).

"So what did Tommy want?" I asked.

B.C. frowned up at me. "Tommy wanted to know what you've done with his sister Jen."

9

"Tommy Zucker wants to know what *I've* done with Jen?" I asked. "That's weird. Did you tell him she's not here?"

B.C. looked up from his bottle cap war and nodded. "But he said *you* shouldn't be here either. You should be with Jen."

"*I* shouldn't be here—?" Then it hit me. Jen's book! I'd totally forgotten about riding to Daltons with Jen so she could get that library book from Stephen. Surely she hadn't taken Cheyenne out in this blizzard all by herself!

I picked up the phone and dialed the Zuckers.

"Scoop?" B.C. asked, coming around to sit on the sofa. "Tommy said there's an abdominal snowman loose in the blizzard and it goes around shaking windows and doors and trying to get in and give kids stomach aches."

The number rang once. Twice. "B.C., don't listen to everything Tommy Zucker tries to—"

"Tommy's Tatoos," came the voice over the phone.

"Tommy, this is Scoop."

"Hey! What did you do with my sister? Travis made me promise to call your house to find out what time you and Jen left. Jen said you and her were riding to Dalton Stables. How come you didn't go?"

"Tommy, let me talk to your mother," I said, trying to stay calm.

"She's not here. Mom and Dad stayed with Granny and Gramps last night. They just took the triplets and the twins, and we didn't get to go. Travis went to pick them up at the bus station, and he's not back. And tomorrow is Turkey Day!"

"Wait a minute, Tommy," I said, trying to get it straight. "Travis isn't back yet? And your folks are gone? And Jen too?" I asked.

"Yep," Tommy said. I could hear the TV blaring in the background. "So *I'm* in charge."

"You mean that you and Rebecca are there by yourselves?" I tried to remember if I'd left anybody out. Travis, Jen, twins, triplets, Rebecca and Tommy. Nope. That was it.

"We're not all the way alone," Tommy admitted. "Travis brought Stephanie over to watch us while he was going to the bus station. But I'm still in charge," he added quickly. "So where's Jen?"

Jen had counted on me going with her to Daltons. She'd been sick so much lately, I hoped she hadn't tried to ride there on her own, especially with the way Cheyenne had been acting.

"Let me talk to your babysitter, Tommy," I asked.

"She can't come to the phone right now. She's ... tied up."

Knowing Tommy Zucker, that babysitter may actually have been tied up. "Listen, Tommy," I said, feeling my heart speed up, "if you hear from Jen, tell her Orphan and I are on our way to Dalton Stables. And tell Travis what's going on as soon as he gets back."

"I'm not your secretary," Tommy informed me.

I hung up and scrounged for warm, dry clothes. "B.C.," I said, hopping on one foot while I stuck a slightly moist sock on the other foot, "I'm going to Horsefeathers. If Jen's not there, I'll ride to Dalton Stables."

B.C. bolted off the couch as if he'd sat on a wasp. "I'm coming with you!" he screamed.

"No!" I said, searching for my other sock. "You stay here. I'm riding Orphan and—"

"No-o-o-o-o-o-o!" he yelled. "I'm afraid of the ab ... abdomen ... abdominal snowman! I'm coming with you!"

"There's no such thing as an abominable snowman! Tommy Zucker was just trying to scare you. You'll be fine."

Something crashed on our roof and rolled noisily down the side, landing with a boom on the front porch. No amount of talk could convince

B.C. it was just a branch. I knew he'd sneak around and follow me if I didn't take him with me.

"Get bundled up with everything you can find," I ordered. I knew there was no snow creature to fear, but every other fear was fighting for space inside my head. What if Jen had left without me? What if Cheyenne had run away? What if something bad had happened to Travis? And where was Dotty? What if she was stranded in a snow drift in a ditch somewhere?

As I zipped B.C.'s snowsuit for him, I prayed out loud, just like Dotty would have. "Lord, look out for Jen and for Travis and for Dotty ... and for us."

I wished I'd memorized more fear verses from the Bible. All I could think of was the psalm about not fearing evil in the valley of the shadow of death. Then I remembered Pastor Dan teaching us in class that God "defends me from all harm, guards and protects me from all evil." I started to feel better because I knew God would protect me.

B.C. looked like an abominable snowman by the time I got finished bundling him up. He waddled outside behind me and almost tumbled off the porch when a broken shutter slammed behind us.

The wind twirled snow as if God were finger-painting in white. Snow was up to my knees everywhere and much deeper where it drifted. I'd never seen a white-out before, but this had to be one.

It took B.C. and me forever to get to Horsefeathers. I'd smelled my way there as much as anything. Not even Orphan and Moby were standing outside when we trudged up the lane. To get the barn door open, I had to use my boots as shovels and kick away the mound of snow that blocked the entrance.

The barn felt warm enough. Nickers resounded from every stall. I ran up and down the stallway, but Cheyenne wasn't there. I checked the tack room—Jen's saddle was gone. She must have left quite a while before because I couldn't find a single print—hoof or foot—outside the barn. She must have come to Horsefeathers just after B.C. and I left. And it was just like Jen to be so stubborn about getting the library book from Stephen, she would have set out for it without me.

B.C. was sitting on a hay bale, petting Dogless Cat.

"B.C.," I said, putting both hands on his shoulders, "I don't suppose you'd like to stay here while I ride after Jen and Cheyenne?"

B.C. shook his head so violently Dogless retreated to the hayloft.

I bridled Orphan and rubbed her hooves with Vaseline to keep the snow from balling on the bottoms of her hooves. Then I led her out of the barn to the south pasture. It was only a mile and a half to Dalton Stables through the pastures. B.C. and I would have to ride Orphan double. In the paddock, the snow reached to B.C.'s waist. I cupped my hands into a stirrup to boost my brother onto Orphan's back.

"Scoot back, B.C.," I yelled above the howling wind. All around, iced branches snapped. It sounded like giant knuckles cracking.

The snow was so deep I couldn't spring up to Orphan's back. I led her to the fence and climbed on from there. "Hold on!" I yelled.

I felt his head burrow into my back and his arms tighten around my waist. "Come on, Orphan," I murmured, leaning forward. "Find Cheyenne!"

Orphan plodded through the deep snow, unsure of her footing on the hidden frozen ground.

My robber's stocking mask had been too wet, so I had on one of Dotty's old stocking caps. My uncovered face felt frozen. I couldn't have moved my mouth enough to speak. Letting my head drop to Orphan's neck, I rubbed my face into her thick, shaggy winter's coat.

When I looked up again, I was completely lost. Everywhere I turned, there was nothing but speckled whiteness—no Horsefeathers, no Dalton Stables, nothing I could recognize. My stomach lurched, as if I were lost at sea; fear washed over me like seasickness.

But Orphan kept moving steadily ahead. I prayed that she knew where she was going. I lost all track of time and didn't know if seconds or minutes or hours had passed. It might have been afternoon, evening, or midnight.

Suddenly I was thrown forward, onto Orphan's neck. She'd stumbled, then caught herself. I reached back and grabbed B.C.'s leg as he slid halfway down Orphan's side. My hand ached as I grasped B.C.'s slick jacket. He didn't utter a sound. He looked asleep.

"B.C.!" I screamed.

Then my hand went numb, and B.C. slid to the ground. Everything felt slow-motion—B.C. landing in a drift, rolling over and over, me struggling off of Orphan and falling face-first in the snow. I waded to B.C. and pulled him up by his jacket collar. He opened his eyes and seemed surprised to see me.

"B.C.!" I yelled. "Are you okay?"

He nodded. When I let go of him, he stayed on his feet.

"We're almost there!" I shouted, but the words came out muffled.

Orphan hadn't budged from our sides. It took three tries, but I managed to lift B.C. onto Orphan's back. I pulled his hands to her mane. "Hold on!" I screamed.

With one arm flung over Orphan's neck for support, I told her to *go*. But she arched her neck and didn't budge. B.C. must have felt her tense too. His eyes, the only things sticking out of his mummy snowsuit, got huge. Orphan whinnied so loud and so long, my brother shook on her back. She did it again.

Then I heard an answering whinny.

"Cheyenne!" I called. We moved in the direction of the whinny. The sun ... or the moon ... crept out of a cloud above us, and I spotted the Paint standing a few yards off, a gray shadow curtained in white.

I squinted, hoping I was wrong, praying I was wrong, that I just couldn't see through the snow and the drifting winds.

But there stood Cheyenne. She was saddled. She was bridled. But Jen Zucker was not on her.

10

Panic sank into my soul as I tried to run to Cheyenne. Snow that drifted to my waist made me move in slow motion. "Jen! Where are you?" I screamed. This was all my fault! I should have remembered. I should have come with her. What if—

Orphan followed me, snow flying off her forelegs as she lifted one hoof, then the other.

When I got a few feet from Cheyenne, I could see her eyes white with fear. She pivoted and leaped off through the snow. I cupped my hands around my mouth and yelled as loud as I could, "Jen! Jen!"

I heard B.C. yelling from Orphan too, his squeaky "Jen!" getting swallowed by the wind.

Studying the snow for footprints made me blind. I couldn't even make out our own prints in the snow. The blizzard swept over every mark we made.

A whistle came from somewhere off to my left. Again, the shrill through-your-teeth whistle sounded above the wind. It was Jen's whistle!

She's the only girl I know who can whistle like that. Travis taught her when she was 7.

"Jen!" I screamed, plowing through snow, following the whistle. B.C. and Orphan stayed so close to me, I could feel Orphan's breath on my neck. "We're coming!"

I tripped over something and fell face-down in the snow. Orphan stopped in time to keep from running over me. Inches from my nose something moved—something green, something soft—an arm. Jen Zucker, in a green down jacket, scooted back in the snow. I threw my arms around her, thanking God for answering prayers I hadn't even had the good sense to pray consciously.

I leaned back and peered into Jen's white face and blue lips, surrounded by a green hood. She was sitting cross-legged inside a kind of snow shelter she must have built around her. "Jen, are you all right?"

Her bluish lips parted in a sickly smile. "Thank heavens you came!" she said, her voice weak and airy. Then she coughed, a deep, rattling cough.

"How long have you been out here?" I asked. How could I have forgotten to meet her?

"I have no idea," Jen said, brushing off snow and working herself out of her half-igloo. "Did you see Cheyenne? Is she all right?"

"We saw her," I said, "but she wouldn't let

me near her."

"It's so ridiculous, Scoop! Cheyenne got spooked when a limb fell in front of us. I wasn't ready for it, and I flew off. It was my fault."

"It was *my* fault," I said. "I'm sorry I forgot about riding over here with you." What if Jen had been lying in the snow the same time I was soaking in my warm bath?

"I shouldn't have come at all," Jen said. "I did something to my ankle when I fell." She winced when she tried to move it. "I don't think I can walk on it." She moved to her other foot. "I think I might have frostbite too. Can you help me up?"

I put her arm around my shoulder and took hold of her hand. My fingers wouldn't bend right. It was like trying to hold a pencil between two tree trunks.

Orphan stuck her head down between us.

"Thanks for the rescue, Orphan," Jen said. "B.C., is that you up there?"

B.C. didn't answer, but he might have nodded his head. I couldn't see him. It took all my powers of concentration to get Jen to a standing position. Jen held on to Orphan's neck, and we got her standing on one foot.

Something dropped in the snow. "My journal!" Jen exclaimed. "Get it!"

Jen held onto my shoulder as I leaned over to retrieve a chunky brown book. I shook snow off of it and handed it to her. "Thanks, Scoop," she said, stuffing it back in her coat pocket.

I'd never known anybody who kept a *journal*. Well, I guess I did know somebody. I just hadn't known about her journal. I wondered what she wrote in there. Maybe Maggie and Carla kept secret journals too. Or maybe I was the only one who didn't know about them, so they weren't all that secret.

"Scoop," Jen said, groaning as she hopped on one foot. "What do we do now?"

"I need to get you up on Orphan," I said. I couldn't imagine how we'd pull it off, but there was no way Jen could make it on foot.

"We're too far away to go back to Horse-feathers," Jen said. "I'm pretty sure the Dalton place is just over that hill." She jerked her chin forward to point.

I held my hands together like a stirrup and tried to give Jen a boost up on Orphan, but her bad ankle couldn't support her weight. "B.C.," I said, trying not to sound as scared as I felt, "I need your help down here."

"Down there?" His body went as rigid as a pine post, but he swung his leg over and slid to the ground. After about a hundred failed attempts to get Jen on Orphan, I got down on my hands and knees in the snow. I felt as if I might drown in snow. B.C. helped Jen balance and get her good foot on my back. Orphan didn't move as Jen flopped her belly over Orphan's back and swung her right leg over.

Holding B.C.'s hand with my left hand and Orphan's reins with my right, I followed Orphan's lead, and we set off into the white blankness. I don't know how long we walked like that, stopping after every couple of steps for B.C. to catch up. But finally I spotted a faint yellowish halo ahead.

"It's the light at Dalton Stables!" I screamed. We aimed for the light, and the stables came into view. Never had that place looked so good.

It took me a couple of minutes to get the stable door unlatched, a few more to kick the snow away. Finally, the door slid back, and a rush of warm air flowed over us. Orphan brought Jen in. Then B.C. and I pulled the door shut against the wind.

We helped Jen off Orphan. She winced when her foot touched the floor, then settled onto a wooden bench set next to the indoor arena. That indoor arena was the only thing I envied at Dalton Stables, and even it was ruined by the sight of two hot-walkers in the middle. They looked like giant wheels with the rims kicked off. A horse could be tied in the walker and made to walk in little circles over and over and over. They call it exercise and do it because they don't feel like riding the horse for real. It's got to be more boring than a treadmill.

As always, the antiseptic stench of Dalton Stables made me gag. It was as if we'd entered a hospital instead of a barn. The stallway was twice as wide and maybe three times as long as at Horsefeathers. Instead of straw on the stall floors, chewed-up rubber had been scientifically mixed with reddish sawdust.

"I need to get to a phone," I said, trying to think. Jen needed help fast. "The Daltons can call somebody to come get us."

"I think I better just sit here for a minute," Jen said weakly.

Bang! Crash! One of the horses kicked against his stall. I ran to see what was wrong. In the first stall Champion, Stephen Dalton's prize American Saddle Horse, charged at me as I went by.

"Easy, boy," I said, but I kept moving. His ears were laid back flat, and he looked like he'd love to take a bite out of me.

"Careful!" Jen hollered. "These aren't backyard horses, Scoop."

She was right about that. Stall after stall held show horses and thoroughbreds, each one wearing a stable blanket, even though the barn was warmer than my house. I came to the beautiful, gray Arabian mare who was kicking her stall door.

"They're out of hay!" I yelled back to Jen.

"I think they're hungry. B.C., see if you can find the oats."

In the stall next to the Arabian, a chestnut thoroughbred mare paced in her little stall. She was so pregnant she could barely make the turn between paces. It was weird to see a horse this far along in November. Somebody's stallion must have got loose.

That's what had happened with Orphan. One of Grandad's prized mares broke loose and found some stallion. Grandad said it ruined thoroughbreds to have half-breed foals. That's why I'd gotten to keep the foal.

"How's this?" B.C. proudly held out a fancy, bright blue scoop, filled with oats. "They got barrels of it in a whole room of horse food!"

"Good job, B.C.," I said. "Give them each a scoop in their feed troughs. Don't get close to Champion. I'll get Orphan settled in an empty stall." I must have been thawing out because my fingers and feet felt like a million pins were being stuck in my flesh.

"I'm *really* hungry too," B.C. whined.

I hurried back to Jen, who still sat slumped on the bench. She coughed and sniffed constantly. I sat down beside her.

"Jen," I said, scared of the way her eyes looked, like the whites had gone yellow and the blue had turned gray. "Do you feel strong enough to come with me to the house?"

"I think I should wait here," she said. She sneezed. "You don't need me dragging you down. Go ahead and get help. I'm okay here."

I didn't want to leave her, but she was right. And the barn was warm. "I'll go tell the Daltons what's going on. They can help us get you inside, and we'll phone for help."

"And eat!" B.C. interrupted.

Jen nodded, and I felt an urgency, like some worry speeding up inside of me, growing bigger.

B.C. insisted on coming with me. It took both of us to push the stable door open. Snow had blown up against it that fast. I knew the Dalton's house was only yards away, but I couldn't make out a trace of it. We leaned into the wind, B.C. following behind me, stepping into my bootprints.

One outside lamp dropped snow-speckled light on the huge porch columns. That's where I aimed us. Snow covered the steps, making it look like the whole porch was ground level. We plowed up five or six hidden steps to the front door. Not a single icicle hung from their porch.

I rang the doorbell. Nobody answered. I rang it again. Still no answer.

My heart beat faster. They had to be home. How could they be gone? They couldn't just leave everything, could they? I moved to a window and peered in. B.C. rang the doorbell over and over while I pressed my nose to the storm windows.

The room was dark. I could see deep into the living room and through two doors, one leading to the hall and the other one to the dining room.

"I'm walking around the house, B.C.," I said. "Maybe they're asleep. Keep ringing the doorbell."

Fear gathered in my throat and stayed there, making it hard for me to swallow, hard to breathe. What if the Daltons really were gone? What on earth would we do then?

After peering into more than a dozen windows, I gave up hoping somebody was home. All I wanted was an open window, an unlocked door. But the house was shut tight.

B.C. was pounding on the front door with both fists when I got back. "Let me in! Let me in!" he screamed. He glanced at me, but didn't stop pounding the door. "I want in!"

All I needed was for B.C.'s manic to kick in, the wild side of his manic depression. "B.C.," I said, trying to sound calm. "It's okay. They must be gone. That's all."

He wheeled around to face me. "They *can't* be gone! What are we going to do? I'm freezing and hungry, Scoop! What are we going to do now?"

"Well," I said, only deciding in that very second I said it, "we're going to break in."

Father, I prayed, searching around for a limb

big enough to break a window, *I'm awful sorry for what I'm about to do. Please help me do it. I don't mean it as a break-in. I just don't see how else to get to a phone. So I hope You understand.*

Right then I stepped on a limb three times the size of my arm. *Thank You, Lord,* I prayed, wrestling it out of snow. *I'll take that as You understanding.*

The ice-covered tree limb was as heavy as a sack of feed. I heaved it over my shoulder and trudged to the front window. It was a tall window, like in pictures of Southern mansions, starting just off the floor and going higher than a body could reach.

"Stand back, B.C.!" I hollered. Squaring myself to the lower windowpane, I took a couple of practice swings, baseball style. Then I tried it in ramming position. Finally, I closed my eyes, swung the limb back behind my shoulder and brought it forward with all my might.

Crash! The window cracked, shattered, and jingled as chunks of glass dropped and clattered onto the sill. Other shards were swallowed up by the snow. A piece of bark fell from my battering limb, and I used it to knock off glass from the top of the sill to make the hole bigger.

B.C. stayed back out of the way as I tossed the limb off the porch. "I'll come around and unlock the door," I whispered to B.C., as if we really were breaking in.

Carefully I braced my hands on the windowsill and stepped one leg through the window. I stretched my toe down, poking my foot around until I felt the carpet under my boot. I ducked, swung my other leg in, and found myself in the Daltons' fancy living room.

The darkness seemed total after the bright snowlight outdoors. I closed my eyes to try to get them used to inside.

Something shuffled behind me. I tried to turn around, but before I could, a shadow moved. And something—somebody—clobbered me over the head. My knees buckled, and everything went black.

11

I may have "come to" before I landed on the thick carpet. I rolled over on my back to face my attacker. Then I heard a scream. And the air was filled with words:

"You big, mean robber! You hurt my sister! I hate you! I hate you! What did you do to Scoop? You killed her! Get out! I hate you!"

"B.C.?" I said, touching the bump on the back of my head. "What's—?"

"Get him off!" Stephen Dalton cowered next to B.C. He was covering his head with his arms. Beside him lay the lamp he'd clobbered me with.

B.C. charged him again, fists raised.

"It's okay, B.C.," I said. The lump at the base of my head was the size of a sugar cube. It hurt to touch it, but otherwise I felt okay. I got to my feet.

B.C. hugged me so hard I almost toppled over again. "I thought he killed you!" he cried.

"Why did you do that, Stephen?" I asked, still trying to get my wits back. "That really hurt!

Didn't you hear the doorbell?"

"I didn't know it was you," Stephen said, his voice a whine. "How was I supposed to know? I'm here all by myself. Didn't you hear about the two convicts who escaped from the state prison this morning? It's all over the news. You could have been them."

"Where's your mother?" I asked, rubbing my sore head and glancing around the huge room.

"She and my dad are at my grandmother's in Ashland. They wanted to have Thanksgiving there. But I refuse to go to Grandmother's house. It's boring. And it smells like cats. So they went to pick her up, but now they're stuck there and I'm stuck here all alone, with two convicts on the loose." He said it in one long whine.

I shook my head at Stephen, and he backed up as if he thought I might hit him back. His foot crunched glass, and he flapped his arms to keep his balance.

"You broke our window!" he cried, as if he'd just noticed.

"Good!" I said. "You broke my head."

"And my mother will be furious about this lamp!"

"You should have thought of that before you tried to kill me with it," I said, prying B.C.'s fingers off my waist.

My eyes had adjusted to the inside, and

Stephen Dalton came into focus. He was dressed in a checkered shirt, gray wool pants, gray wool socks, and a matching gray vest—dressed up like that to sit around home alone! Stephen's mother and my dad were sister and brother, but I would never understand Stephen or any of the Daltons—never.

I could tell by Stephen's tight thin lips, his beady green eyes, and the way he tipped his pointy chin that he'd really been scared. Good.

Stephen hugged himself and shivered. "You're dripping water all over the carpet. And cold air is getting in through the broken window," he whimpered, smoothing down his oily, red hair.

"We'll fix it later," I said. "Right now, you're going to get your coat and boots on and get out to the stable. Jen Zucker is out there—"

"Jen Zucker?" Stephen squealed. "What's *she* doing there? What are *you* doing here, for that matter?"

"Listen to me, Stephen, or I'll break a dozen lamps over *your* head!" I commanded. God knew I wouldn't do that, but maybe Stephen didn't know. "Jen is sick." Even saying it out loud made me more afraid for her. For weeks I'd had a feeling something was really wrong with Jen, but she kept saying she had a cold or hadn't gotten enough sleep or was just getting over the flu. Still, I wondered if Jen might be hiding something.

"Stephen Dalton," I said calmly through clenched teeth, "Jen Zucker is out there by herself in *your* barn. And *you* are going out there right this very minute and bring her inside. Do you understand?"

"Why does she have to come in here?" Stephen asked, taking another step backward and away from me. "You can't stay here, you know. I'm not allowed to have guests when my parents are away, especially not girls."

"Do you even realize there's a blizzard outside?" I shouted in his face, matching him step for step. "Jen can't walk. She hurt her ankle. Now go! You'll have to carry her. And be careful!"

Stephen sputtered like a stalled engine, but he got his coat and boots on and unlocked the front door. "It's freezing out there!" he cried as he stepped out onto the porch.

"No kidding, Stephen," I said. "We hadn't noticed."

B.C. slammed the front door behind Stephen. Then we yanked a cover off one of the couches and tucked it around the top of the broken window to keep the snow out. But it didn't work great. The blanket flapped in the wind, and cold air still poured in.

I watched from the window as Stephen made his way down the hill to the stables. The short journey took him a hundred times longer than it had taken us to come up the hill. "Go!" I muttered under my breath. Visions of Jen, unconscious, passed out on the stable floor, flooded my mind. *Lord,* I prayed, *what's the matter with Jen? Make her be okay.*

Finally I saw the light inside the stable as Stephen wrestled the sliding door back. He left it open, and I couldn't see anything. My stomach churned as I tried to make out something, anything, through the white fog that swirled with huge snowflakes.

"Cool!" B.C. exclaimed from somewhere behind me. "Look at the size of this TV, Scoop! And wow! Get a load of these! I wonder how much this costs? Dotty would love this!"

"Careful, B.C.," I said, without turning away from the window. I thought I saw something. Then I did for sure. They were coming out of the barn. "All right, Stephen!" I whispered.

Through the blowing snow, I could only see a dark figure carrying something out in front of him. The figure wobbled, zigzagged through the snow, stopped, started up again. My heart raced and strained with the effort, as if I were the one carrying Jen up the hill. I couldn't see her very well, couldn't tell if she was moving or kicking or talking, or just lying there. "Come on," I muttered. "You can do it."

Something clattered behind me. B.C. let out an, "Oops. Sorry."

I ran over and helped B.C. pick up the dozen or so candles he'd knocked off the fireplace mantel.

"I'm sorry. I'm sorry," said B.C., sounding scared. "I didn't mean to do it. Will Steve be mad? Do you think Steve will hit *me* over the head with a lamp?"

"Not a chance, B.C.," I said, grinning at the way my brother reduced Stephen Dalton to just plain Steve. I liked it. "Besides, you didn't really hurt anything."

A couple of the candles were broken, but they didn't fall apart. I tried to make them stand up straight again on the mantel. I wondered how much allowance it would take to replace the broken ones. The gold, jeweled candles didn't look like the candles Dotty brought home from Hy-Klas to have on hand in case the electricity went out.

Before I could run back to my post at the window, I heard them at the front door. "Jen!" I cried, throwing open the huge, solid wood door that was twice as big as a normal door. "Are you okay?"

Jen smiled at me. "I don't think I've got frostbite, so that's good. Stephen is very upset that the Dalton show horses are under the same roof as a Horsefeathers' backyard horse, aren't you, Stephen?" She looked so tiny, like she wouldn't weigh more than a horse's tail. But

Stephen was huffing and puffing as if he'd carried Orphan in instead of Jen.

Stephen struggled past me so I could close the door. They were both white as snowmen. Even Stephen's red hair had turned white, an improvement. "Where—*huff, puff*—should—*gasp, heave*—I put—?"

The phone rang, and B.C. got it before the second ring, and before Stephen hollered, "Don't! *I'll* get it!"

"Hi!" B.C. said into the fancy gold-mouthed telephone that looked kind of like our old black one. This phone sat on a fancy table that looked like a large musical note made of wood. You could tell the phone was new and expensive, but made to look like an old time telephone. Stuff like that always makes Dotty laugh—people paying lots of money to have things look like they were old. I sent up a quick prayer that Dotty would be safe, wherever she was.

"I'm B.C.," said my brother, after a pause that must have filled with somebody asking who's this.

"He can't come to the phone right now," B.C. said, glancing over at us.

"Wait!" Stephen shouted, swinging Jen left, then right, looking for a place to dump her. "Who is it?"

"Because he's got his hands full," B.C. explained to the caller.

"I'm coming!" Steven cried, crossing the huge marble entrance I knew they called a foyer.

"Full of what?" B.C. said, stepping up into an adjoining room. He plopped into a recliner next to a big, stone fireplace. "His hands are full of girl, I guess."

"B.C.!" Stephen demanded. "Who is it?"

"Jen Zucker is in his arms so he can't hold the phone," B.C. explained.

Stephen took four giant steps to the couch and dropped Jen so hard she bounced on the plush, white cushions. Not one speck of dust flew up.

"Wait!" Stephen shouted, stumbling into an end table. "I'm—"

But B.C. hung up. "That wasn't very nice," B.C. said. "I think she hung up on me."

"She?" Stephen asked, frantically picking up the phone, putting it to his ear, then hanging up. "She who?"

B.C. leaned back hard in the recliner and seemed surprised when the footstool popped out. "I don't know for sure, Steve," he said absently, obviously already moving on in his mind to the wonders of the Dalton mansion.

"She must have said something!" Stephen screamed down at him. "Think! What did she say? Who was it?"

B.C. frowned up at Stephen, his face wrinkling like an old man's. "Purse—no, that wasn't it. It was a funny name. *Hearse?* No, that's not it. It was *Hurl-something* though."

Ursula! I glanced at Jen, and could see by her mischievous grin she understood the same second I did. Ursula is Stephen's girlfriend. She can be just as stuck up as he can.

"B.C.," Stephen said, holding his head in his hands, as if *he* had just been bonked over the head with an expensive lamp. "Tell me it wasn't Ursula!"

"That's it, Steve," B.C. said. "I don't think she's in a good mood. She talks mean. You got something to eat, Steve? I'm starving."

12

"You little—you just hung up on Ursula?" Stephen's nostrils grew wide as quarters. I half-expected to see flames shoot out his ears. "My girlfriend?"

"Sorry," B.C. said simply. "Maybe you should get a nicer girlfriend, Steve."

I burst out laughing.

"And stop calling me *Steve!*"

I didn't like the way Stephen yelled at my little brother. "Lay off B.C., *Steve,*" I yelled back. But Jen and I were laughing so hard, he probably couldn't understand me.

It was good to hear Jen laugh. Travis teases his sister that it's a good thing she isn't fat because she's not at all jolly. Jen is never bad tempered. She's just not a laugher by nature, and lately not at all.

I threw myself down on the floor by the sofa where Jen lay, still shaking with laughter. I laughed so hard tears blurred my vision. Then Jen's laugh changed to a cough. And the cough rattled around inside her so hard, I stopped laughing too.

"My name is *Stephen!*" Stephen yelled, inches from B.C.'s puzzled face. "*Stee*-ven! *Stee*-ven!"

"Sorry, *Stee*-ven," B.C. said, seriously mimicking the way Stephen said it. B.C. wasn't even trying to be funny, but Jen and I busted out into laughing fits all over again.

Stephen was sputtering with rage. "I'll call Ursula back myself and—"

Before Stephen could finish his sentence or pick up the phone, it rang again.

"I'll get it, Stee-ven!" B.C. called, reaching for the phone.

"Oh no you don't!" cried Stephen, tripping over a footstool to grab the phone. "Hello!" he said into the receiver, steadying himself on the musical table. An ashtray slid off, and he made a diving catch to save it. "Ursula, let me explain! I didn't—"

Stephen stopped and frowned. "Maggie 37?"

Jen and I exchanged looks. Then she slapped her forehead as if she'd forgotten something.

"What?" I asked Jen.

"Scoop," Jen said. "I'm sorry."

"Yes," Stephen answered into the phone. "How did you know they were here?" He shot us hateful glares. "Okay, okay! Keep your shirt on! I'll get her." He put his hand over the mouthpiece, as if he didn't want Maggie to hear. "Scoop, it's for you."

I jumped up, amazed Maggie knew where to find me.

Stephen held out the gold telephone. "Keep it short," he said, sounding disgusted. "I have to call Ursula back."

"Maggie?" I asked into the phone.

"Scoop, how could y'all be at Stephen Dalton's still?" Maggie's southern accent shouted above crowd noises in the background. It sounded like a room full of rowdy kids. I thought I heard Carla's voice and Brian's.

"Maggie, what's going on?" I asked, looking over at Jen, who mouthed the word *sorry*.

"Isn't Jen there with you?" Maggie asked. "Didn't she tell you why she wanted you to ride over there with her? Why *today?*"

"I guess she wanted the library book Stephen had—"

"Hey! Pipe down, y'all!" Maggie shouted. "I can't hear!" Then she said into the phone, "Jen was supposed to distract you while the rest of us got everything ready. Scoop, it's ... Scoop, it's your birthday party!"

"Happy Birthday!" "Happy Birthday to you!" "Scoop, happy birthday!" The half-howls, half-songs screeched across the phone lines through the receiver. I might have heard Ray's low voice, but I couldn't make out the others.

"*My* birthday party?" I asked, still not quite getting it.

"Yes! Your party!" said Maggie 37. "Jen was supposed to get you here by six o'clock. None of the country kids could make it in, of course. Just the kids who live in town and could walk here. When can you get here?"

"Maggie," I said, so frustrated I could hardly stand it, "we *can't* get there. We can't get anywhere! We're stuck. Snowbound. Trapped—at least until somebody comes for us."

"But it's *your* party!" she cried.

I should have felt great that somebody had remembered, that a whole party had been planned for me. But all I could feel was how unfair this was—my only real birthday party since my seventh birthday, and I wasn't even there. I ached inside hearing them laughing and joking in the background. They were sure having a great time without me.

I'd only been 15 for one day, and already it stank.

"Let me talk to Jen," Maggie said.

I stretched the phone cord, plopped down beside the couch, and handed the phone to Jen, glad to get rid of it before I burst out crying.

"I know, Maggie. I know," Jen said. "I thought I had it all worked out to get Scoop there. It's a long story. ... Wow! Sounds like everybody but us made it. Don't tell me. I know

I hear Ray, Carla, Alison, Katy, Brent, Brian, Dan." Jen can identify people by their laughs, which I always thought was weird since she doesn't let us hear *her* laugh all that often. "Did your mom help you frost the cake, Maggie?"

I had to get out of there.

I got up and found Stephen's coat thrown over the back of a chair. Then I rummaged through a box in the hall closet until I came out with dry gloves and a hat. "I'm going out to find Cheyenne," I said.

"That's my coat!" Stephen yelled. He was sitting on the staircase, looking down on us and pouting.

"Mine is too wet," I said, not mentioning that his coat looked 10 times warmer than mine. "B.C., call home when Jen gets off. And tell Jen to call her folks too. Maybe Travis can come get us."

Jen said something to me, but I kept going, pretending not to hear. I wanted to be in my own home. I missed Dotty. I should have tried to call her myself, but I was afraid of what she'd have to say. What if she'd gone to Cinnamon Lake and found such a great job she'd never come back?

My tears froze on my cheeks the minute I stepped outside. I'd never seen this much snow. The wind tore at Stephen's coat before I could get it buttoned. A bright, nearly full moon made the snow shimmer like the silver glitter B.C. spilled all over the living room when he was 5 years old and didn't want to start kindergarten. Every now and then a speck of glitter still turned up in the carpet.

I wanted to pray, but I didn't know where to start. If Dotty had been there, the prayers would have fallen as freely as the snow, covering everything as natural as sundown. Dotty always says God reads our hearts and knows our fears. I hoped God was reading mine because I couldn't seem to put my fears into words. Inside I was scared for Dotty, for B.C. and me, for Jen, for Cheyenne. And I felt like crying because instead of being at my own birthday party, I was in the place I'd least like to be, Dalton Stables.

Orphan was glad to see me. As soon as I caught sight of her in the stall, some of the swirling feelings inside of me settled, like the fake snow inside B.C.'s little Christmas snow shaker.

I scratched Orphan's jaw, grinning at her winter whiskers and fur-lined ears. She looked as out of place in the Dalton Stables as I felt in the Dalton mansion. None of the other horses in the stable had thick, furry coats like Orphan's because the Dalton grooms kept stable blankets on them.

The pregnant mare seemed ready to burst. She let me scratch her back, and she ate from my hand as if she hadn't eaten for weeks. The horses boarded at Dalton Stables couldn't even see their neighbors in adjacent stalls. Black iron grates topped every wooden partition between the small stalls. The whole stables had the feel of a horse prison. I wondered if the Dalton inmates ever got outside to play in the snow.

I slipped Orphan a handful of oats and led her out of the stall to the stable door. Once outside, I swung myself up on her bareback. "Find Cheyenne," I told Orphan.

Having no idea where the Paint might be, I let Orphan go wherever she wanted. She headed downhill, behind the stable, making her path as confidently as if she were following a horse map. I was sure no Thanksgiving had ever brought so much snow, not in our state anyway.

Thanksgiving. What was Thanksgiving going to be like? I had to get home. I didn't care if we didn't get a turkey or stuffing or anything. I just wanted Dotty and B.C. and me in our own home.

I could still make out the faint glow of the stable light behind us when Orphan stopped and let out a long whinny. The night felt padded, muffled, and only a faint echo answered us. Again, she neighed long and loud, shaking my whole body as her chest heaved out in sharp blasts.

This time we got an answer. Only a few yards away, Cheyenne appeared like a phantom in the blizzard, B.C.'s abdominal snowman. Orphan stayed where she was, and Cheyenne came to us, covered with tiny icicles that dangled from her shaggy coat. Snow clumped on her saddle and blanket and matted her mane and forelock.

She tagged along behind Orphan all the way back to Dalton Stables. I slid off my horse, shoved the door back, and stood aside. Orphan walked in, but Cheyenne stopped, unsure, snorting, ready to bolt.

Usually I know what to do when a horse is frightened. But this time I didn't. Maybe it was because I was so filled with my own fears. Everything I'd touched lately had turned out wrong. How could I expect Cheyenne to trust me when I wasn't sure I could trust myself?

But Orphan took over, turning back to face Cheyenne, and nickering secret promises to her until the Paint leaped through the entrance and trotted down the stallway of Dalton Stables.

I shoved the door closed and waited until Cheyenne settled down before leading her into an empty stall and unsaddling her.

I finished grooming Cheyenne, brushed Orphan again, and gave the other horses hay.

What if we really were trapped here? What if nobody could come get us? My throat felt tight, and my head hurt from trying to hold back tears. What if I had to go to sleep on my birthday and wake up on Thanksgiving Day—in the Dalton mansion?

Walking down the stallway to the end stall, where the pregnant mare pawed nervously, I thought about Jen. She didn't want to be at the Daltons any more than I did. And she just didn't look good. I thought about how often she'd been sick over the past few months. She'd missed a lot of school—a lot for her anyway. Jen loved school. I prayed and asked God to look out for Jen.

The mare sidled up to me so I'd scratch her again. Her belly moved, and she groaned. That foal inside couldn't wait to come out.

"You don't want to come out in this weather," I told the foal. "Couldn't you wait until spring to be born, like normal horses?"

The poor mare paced the stall restlessly. I'd have to ask Stephen when she was due to foal.

I hurried back up the stallway, giving Orphan and Cheyenne good-night strokes. Near the door, I stopped to admire Champion's silky mane and his perfect confirmation.

"You're a beauty," I said, admiring the arch of the five-gated sorrel gelding's neck as he took a step toward me.

Before I could step away, Champion lunged at me, head stretched forward, teeth bared. All I saw was a flash of white as his teeth clamped onto my right forearm.

I screamed, falling backward from the surprise of it. He didn't let go. I heard the jacket rip. Then I felt a throbbing pain that brought stinging tears to my eyes.

I jerked my arm away and grabbed my forearm. I couldn't see anything through the jacket, but I knew he'd drawn blood—and probably left a honey of a bruise. What was wrong with me? I can always read when a horse is about to bite.

I left the stable and trudged through the snow as it kept falling in the eerie moonlight.

And that's when I heard screams coming from the Dalton house. They were loud enough to wake the dead.

13

I hurried through the snow to the door and made my way inside the Dalton mansion. I half-expected to see Stephen's escaped convicts.

What I found in the living room was a scene as wild as the snowstorm outside. Jen Zucker was screaming over the phone: "Tommy Zucker, you hang up this instant and untie that babysitter!"

Drowning out Jen's cries was a multitude of TV voices:

"And in the Pacific Northwest, rains have—"

"Stay tuned for an all-new episode of—"

"Screeech! Crash! Whoo-whoo—"

"Early this morning two convicts escaped from the state prison facility of—"

"Leave the channel there, B.C.!" Stephen shouted, chasing my brother around the phone and Jen, behind the couch, past the foyer.

B.C. could never sit still long enough to watch a whole TV show, and the Dalton's remote control must have pushed him over the edge. He sped by me, remote held in front of him like a divining rod, changing channels every second.

"Scoop!" B.C. yelled. "You're safe! Dotty's not home!" But he didn't slow down, and neither did Stephen, who stayed in hot pursuit. B.C. slipped on an Oriental rug. Then Stephen slipped too, crashing into a footstool.

They came around again, knocking over a stack of books Jen had already piled beside the couch. "Look how huge those bad men are!" B.C. yelled as he slid past me. "Can't catch me, *Stee*-ven!" he taunted.

I turned to look at what I'd first thought was a big-screen TV. Now the two cabinets that flanked the center screen were shoved back to reveal two more screens, taking up the whole wall between windows. The picture was as big as the one in the Hamilton movie theater. But from my angle, all I could see were little gray and white dots. The TV screen flashed on and off, changing the shadows of the whole room.

Jen was screaming louder into the phone. "Go get Travis, Tommy! I mean it!"

Stephen huffed and gasped, breathless from the chase. He slid to a stop in front of me. "Make B.C. give me the remote control!" he demanded.

B.C. kept circling, swerving out of Stephen's reach as he thundered by. "Look, Scoop! They get a zillion TV stations!" He proved it, flashing from one to the next, as Stephen took up the chase again.

My arm must have been thawing out because the tingles turned to pounding throbs. I tried to unbutton the coat to check out the damage. I knew something was sticking to the wound.

"SCOOP!" Jen must have been yelling for a while, trying to get my attention from across the room. When I looked over, she waved the phone at me, motioning me to join her.

B.C. took the stairs, with Stephen close behind. "You're not allowed up there!" Stephen shouted.

"You got any bottle caps up here? I left my bottle caps home!" B.C. shouted.

On the TV screen, somebody was diving into a clear, blue swimming pool.

Jen, her ear to the phone, raised her eyebrows at me. Her blue eyes looked gray, and the circles I'd seen under her eyes had turned into dark shadow pools. "Scoop's back, Travis." She focused on me. "Did you find Cheyenne?"

"She's fine," I said. "I put her in the stall next to Orphan. Can Travis come get us?"

Jen shook her head. "He barely made it home from the bus station. His truck got stuck, and he had to walk over a mile. My parents stayed at Granny's. They never made it to the bus." She frowned, listening to Travis on the other end of the line. "Scoop's right here." Jen glanced at me, then handed me the phone. "Travis wants to talk to you."

Jen limped to the wall-TV and stooped over the controls. Suddenly the blaring racket died, and B.C.'s voice came down from upstairs, "Ha! Missed me!"

I pressed the receiver to my ear and discovered I still had the stocking cap on. I pulled it off, sending snow flying everywhere. "Travis?"

"Scoop! Are you okay?" Travis' warm, worried voice made me want to cry. "I can't believe this!"

I tried to make my voice stop shaking. "I'm okay, I guess. B.C. said Dotty's not home though. She was going to Cinnamon—"

"Dotty's okay," Travis said, interrupting. "When she couldn't reach you at home, she called Pastor Dan. And he called over here. Your aunt is safe. She's still in Cinnamon Lake. So many of the roads are closed. Nobody expected this much snow so early."

I told God thanks for keeping Dotty safe. But even before I'd finished praying, a fear rose from deep inside me. "So Dotty ... stayed there?" I asked Travis. "In Cinnamon Lake?"

"Yeah," he said. "She was calling from her friend's house, her old boss—can't remember the name. She was glad you and B.C. are okay."

"Was she ... did she say when she'd be coming back?" I tried to sound regular, even though my heart pounded faster than horse hooves at full gallop.

"I don't know, Scoop. Even the interstate's closed in places. I could hear her friend in the background telling her she'd better plan on staying over."

"Isn't there anybody who can get us?" My throat burned from all I wasn't saying. I wanted to go home. I wanted Dotty home too.

"Not tonight, Scoop," Travis said gently. "You and Jen and B.C. just stay there where it's safe and warm."

I didn't answer, afraid of what I might say.

"Scoop?" Travis said it in a whisper. "Listen, how is Jen ... really?"

I glanced at her. She'd gone back to the couch and had two books open. She stared at one, then the other, reading them at the same time. "I think she's fine. She hurt her ankle when she fell," I said.

"I know," Travis said. "But is she—? Does she—?" I could feel him struggling for the right words. "How is she acting, Scoop?"

"What do you mean?"

He sighed and I could almost feel his breath through the phone. "I'm worried about her, Scoop."

So I wasn't the only one. I wasn't imagining it. I lowered my voice. "Jen looks sick, Travis.

And she's tired, really tired. But she's jumpy too. What's wrong with her?"

"I wish I knew," he said, matching my whisper so I could hardly hear him.

Neither of us said anything for a few seconds. Fear tightened my chest so I had to take a deep breath to get any air in.

"Scoop," Travis said at last, "I don't know what's going on with Jen, but I know it's something. And it's not good. She won't talk to me—snaps my head off if I ask her anything. And all she does is write in that diary of hers."

I glanced at Jen again, and she was picking up her journal and feeling around for a pen.

"Scoop?" Travis sounded like he thought I'd hung up.

"I'm here," I said.

"Find out what's going on with her. Something is wrong. Maybe she'll talk to you about it."

"Horsefeathers, Travis!" I said. I lowered my voice. "Me? What would I say?"

"If I knew the right thing to say, I wouldn't have to ask you," he answered. "But I'll be praying God gives you the right words. We've got to help her, Scoop. Jen is hiding something. And I can't get through to her. Maybe you can."

"Mine! Mine! Mine! Mine!" B.C. thundered down the stairs, clutching the remote to his heart.

"I've gotta go," I told Travis. We hung up.

"B.C.!" I commanded. "Give me that." I held out my hand.

B.C. shrugged. "Okay. I'm starving. I need a sandwich." When B.C. says it, it sounds like *sammich*. "A ham sammich." He strolled off toward the kitchen as if the last hour had never happened.

Stephen plodded down the stairs. His shirt was splotched with sweaty underarms, and his pants wrinkled. His hair looked like someone had cracked an egg over it. He plopped into the chair next to me and looked up.

His eyes narrowed, and he stretched his skinny neck toward me, his beak-nose only inches from my aching arm. "Hey!" he shouted. "What did you do to my coat?"

"Me?" I asked, gingerly touching the sore part. "What did *I* do to your coat?"

"You're going to pay for that! That's a $500 coat!" He acted like he was going to rip it right off me.

"*Your* horse did that," I said, trying to shrug out of the coat. "Champion took a chunk out of your coat and my arm."

"Scoop?" Jen called over. "Are you all right? Come over here and let me look at your arm."

I obeyed, glad to have help getting out of the coat. "I should have seen it coming," I said. "But that horse always looks like he's ready to take a chunk out of me." It hurt when Jen pulled on the coat but we got it off.

We pushed up the sleeve of my gray sweatshirt. Champion had bitten all the way through to my skin. A semi-circle of teeth had left their mark on my forearm, breaking the skin in three places and bruising the entire top of my arm.

"We need to clean and bandage it," Jen said, pushing my sleeve above my elbow. "Stephen, get some bandages and bring them down."

"Bandages?" Stephen repeated. "I don't know where any bandages are."

Jen scowled at him. "Excuse me?"

"How should I know where they are?" Stephen whined.

"You *do* live here, don't you?" she said.

"You don't have to get all snippy," he said.

Jen sighed. "I've got Band-Aids in my coat pocket, Scoop. Go get those." She called to Stephen, "I know you don't know where antiseptic might be, Stephen. But go to your bathroom—you *do* know where the bathroom is, don't you? Open the medicine cabinet, and bring me anything in a tube or a spray can."

We split up for our assignments. Jen's coat was draped over the hall windowsill. I felt through her coat pockets and found a pen, a nickel, and a frilly handkerchief. In an inside pocket, my hand closed on something cold and hard and wrinkly. I pulled out a lumpy ball of foil about half the size of my fist.

Something was inside the foil. I had no business snooping, but Travis' worried pleas about Jen replayed in my brain. I glanced back over my shoulder. Jen was yelling into the kitchen for B.C. to bring her a wet dishtowel.

Carefully, I unwrapped the aluminum foil package, folding the edges back into a silvery nest. When I pulled away the last crumpled foil covering, I let out a gasp. Inside were pills—small white ones, big yellow ones, red oblong pills, and blue capsules. I had never seen so many pills in one place in my whole life. There was only one explanation.

Jen Zucker was on drugs.

14

My hands shook as I wrapped the pills back up.

"Scoop?" Jen called. "Did you find the Band-Aids?"

I shoved the packet back into her coat pocket. "Uh ... not quite yet." I felt in the side pocket. "Okay! Got 'em!"

I carried two Band-Aids back to the couch, where Jen and B.C. were ready with a wet dishtowel. Jen was still lying on the couch. I didn't want to look her in the face.

Jen Zucker had always been the reliable one. She'd grown up taking care of seven younger siblings. She never forgot a test, always did her homework. She was the president of our church youth group. She had more Bible verses memorized than anybody I knew, except maybe Dotty. And Dotty forgot the exact wording. Jen never did. How could she possibly be on drugs?

"Scoop?" Jen said. "You need to get down where I can reach you." She propped herself up on one elbow, while I knelt in front of her, keeping my head down.

"Can you get your sweatshirt off, or push the sleeve up farther?" She turned to yell toward the stairs, "Stephen Dalton, what are you doing up there? Hurry up!"

A door slammed upstairs, and Stephen came down. "I don't know what you want." He handed over two fistfuls of tubes and a squatty spray can that looked like Dotty's deodorant, but said *First Aid* on the side.

"Good," Jen mumbled, studying the labels.

I racked my brain to remember what the officer who had visited our school in sixth grade had told us about drugs. It was a D.A.R.E. program. I couldn't remember what the initials stood for, but it was all about saying no to drugs. What were the signs that a friend might be on drugs? Tiredness, mood swings, missing classes? Jen had all of that. Why hadn't I suspected anything before?

Because Jen Zucker wouldn't use drugs. That's why. But the officer said anybody could be lured into it.

"Yuk!" B.C. was standing on his tiptoes to look at my wound. "Champion is a mean horse! I hate him!" B.C. cried. "*Stee*-ven has a mean girlfriend and a mean horse! Does it hurt awful, Scoop?"

Before I could answer, B.C. had taken off for

the kitchen. "Where's the hot chocolate? I want hot chocolate. Dotty always makes me hot chocolate! Where is it?"

Other signs of drugs were things like acting secretive, keeping secrets. I had to find a way to make Jen talk to me. I wished Travis were there. I needed help. I couldn't ask Stephen to help me. He'd probably turn Jen in to the police. And B.C. was already well on his way to being manic, which meant he was a loaded cannon looking for a fuse. I didn't want to give him one.

"Ow!" Jen sprayed something on my bite. It felt like icicles digging into my skin. The pain made my eyes water.

"That's to make sure the area doesn't get infected," Jen explained. She handed the can back to Stephen. Then she squeezed white ointment from a silver tube onto one of the Band-Aids.

"This may sting a little," she warned as she pressed the Band-Aid over the worst of the tooth marks.

It stung a lot. "Horsefeathers! That really hurts," I said.

Jen did the same thing with the second Band-Aid so all the cut parts were covered. "There," she said. "Keep these two antiseptics down here," she commanded Stephen, "and take those back. Keep all of them out of B.C.'s reach."

I had to say something, to try something. "Good idea, Jen," I said. "Um ... things like that can really be dangerous."

"I should know." Jen settled back on the couch again. "If something can be gotten into, the twins will get into it. We had to keep the medicine cabinet padlocked when Tommy was little."

"Yeah," I said, still not looking at her. I acted like I was pressing the Band-Aids down. "Because those things are kind of like drugs really. And drugs are so dangerous."

Jen didn't say anything. She closed her eyes and took two deep breaths.

"Remember Officer ... What was his name?" I tried again. "That policeman who came to talk to us in sixth grade? You know, the D.A.R.E. program."

"Officer Shipper," Jen said, not opening her eyes.

"That was a good program," I said.

Jen didn't respond.

Lord Jesus, I prayed, continuing to smooth those Band-Aids that didn't need smoothing, *help me say the right thing. I'm so scared, and I don't even know what I'm scared of. What if I say the wrong thing and push Jen over the edge, or make her mad at me?*

"Jen," I began, "I found—"

"Hot chocolate! Hot chocolate! Hot chocolate!" B.C. darted into the living room and plopped down on the couch, almost landing on Jen.

"Careful, B.C.!" I yelled.

"They don't have anything to eat here and I'm starving!" he said, his words spilling out faster and faster, like snow caught in the wind. "Dotty always makes me hot chocolate at night!" He looked past me and his eyes widened. "It's too dark! I hate dark!"

B.C. jumped up and raced around the room, flipping on switches and clicking on lamps. A huge chandelier in the center of the room came to life and made teardrop shadows on the white carpet—a color that would have lasted about two seconds in our house.

B.C. turned the TV back on, but Jen must have found the mute button because no sound came out. He raced through the dining room, back up the hall to the kitchen, on around the other side of the house. And he flipped on lights everywhere he saw a switch.

Close to the fireplace, Stephen leaned back in a recliner and let out a low moan. He picked up the phone and dialed, then waited. "Hello?" he said into the phone. "Ursula, you have to listen to me. It's not what you think! I didn't have a girl in my arms. I mean, I did, but— Hello? Ursula?"

Stephen slammed down the phone. "She

won't even let me explain," he wailed. He bit into something that looked like a candy bar.

B.C. circled all the rooms again, screaming "Hot chocolate! Hot chocolate!"

And I lost the little bit of nerve I had. I didn't know what to say to Jen. What if I said the wrong thing and just made it all worse?

"Come on, B.C.," I said, putting my hand out to stop him as he stormed past the couch. "Let's see what the Dalton refrigerator looks like."

The Dalton kitchen was approximately the size of Alaska, and the refrigerator would just barely fit in Rhode Island. I pulled open one door, and B.C. pulled the other.

"See?" B.C. said, as we peered into the freezer-refrigerator-ice-and-cold-water-machine. "No hot chocolate in here. And no chocolate pudding. And no pistachio pudding. And look at this!" He held up a tiny container, maybe a quart, of skim, fat-free, *milk*-free milk. "They drink water milk!"

I didn't know anybody really bought milk in those little cartons. Dotty brings home real milk in plastic gallon jugs, two at a time if Hy-Klas runs a sale. Then I remembered. Dotty didn't work at Hy-Klas anymore. I'd gotten her fired.

"Where's the real food?" B.C. asked, his voice shrill and edgy.

Instead of the white Styrofoam containers

we always had in our fridge, or the cold cuts wrapped in the Hy-Klas deli paper, the Dalton shelves were filled with weird things that looked a long way from being food. One whole shelf was filled with funny-shaped bottles: cherries, pickle relish, olives—four jars of olives!—and a bunch of stuff I couldn't pronounce.

"Is this chocolate?" B.C. asked, pulling out a huge jar of something black and speckled.

I read the label. *"Caviar.* It doesn't look very good, does it, B.C.?" I said. "Want to try it anyway?"

"Put back that caviar!" Stephen stormed into the kitchen and grabbed the jar out of my hands. "Are you crazy? That stuff costs more than ... than ... than your horse!" He carefully placed it in the back of the refrigerator.

"Big deal," I muttered. "It looked awful. We didn't want it anyway, did we, B.C.?"

"Maybe it would be good with peanut butter," B.C. suggested. "Like peanut butter and jelly? You got any peanut butter?"

I opened a fridge drawer filled with cheese that smelled old and expensive, but not tasty like Velveeta and Hy-Klas American. The drawer smelled like something had died in it. Shutting it fast, I said, "B.C.'s right. You got any peanut butter?"

Stephen sighed, but didn't answer.

"How about bread?" I asked, willing to

compromise. "Where's the bread?" Sometimes Dotty puts ours in the fridge to make it last longer. I moved other stuff around to find it.

"And the hot chocolate?" B.C. screamed.

On the very top shelf sat the biggest turkey I'd ever seen in my whole life. I poked it. "Are you guys feeding an army or what?" I asked, opening the fridge all the way so Jen, who was leaning in the doorway, could see the monster turkey.

Jen limped over to the fridge. She seemed to be putting more weight on her foot. That was the least of her problems though. "I can't believe this turkey!" she exclaimed, studying it. "You didn't get that around here, did you, Stephen? Now the Zucker clan could actually use a turkey like this. We have to cook two turkeys. But I guess with a turkey even this big, the twins and Tommy would still fight over who gets the drumsticks. Where did you get this monster, Stephen?"

Stephen shrugged. "How should I know? The cook got it, I guess. A lot of good that turkey is going to do any of us now. Even if Mother and Father can start driving here early in the morning, what about the cook? She should be here right now getting the turkey ready for us."

"Yeah, just can't get good help these days, huh, Stephen?" I said. I couldn't imagine what it would be like to have a cook. "She won't even walk over here in a blizzard to make stuffing? I'd fire her."

Jen pushed between B.C. and me. B.C. was pulling out okra and squash and stuff I'd never seen before.

"Stephen," Jen said, in her take-charge voice, "get this bird out of the refrigerator and onto the counter. It's thawed out."

"Why?" Stephen asked, sounding suspicious, like Jen might clobber him with it.

"Do it!" she commanded, and he did. "I need bread, lots of it. And butter, celery—that's it, B.C. And onions."

"You're making stuffing?" I asked, getting as excited as Christmas.

Jen turned around and grinned at me, looking more like the old Jen, the real Jen, than she had for weeks. She almost looked like a different person. Was that one of the drug warning signals?

"And that's not all I'm making," Jen announced.

Stephen and B.C. had all the stuffing ingredients set on the kitchen counter that ran the whole length of two walls. The turkey took up the entire butcher block that sprouted from the center of the kitchen like a giant mushroom.

"Now, I need flour, sugar, butter, eggs, vanilla, cocoa, baking powder and baking soda, salt, powdered sugar, milk." Jen pulled her hair back and retied her ribbon. Then she hobbled over to the sink and started washing her hands.

"What are you making besides turkey?" B.C. asked, copying Jen and washing his hands in the sink beside her.

"Well, B.C.," Jen said, leaning down as if they were plotting something together. "Tomorrow is Thanksgiving, so we need turkey."

"Hey—" Stephen tried to cut in, but I elbowed him into silence.

"And isn't today a special day too?" Jen asked, jerking her head in my direction.

"Scoop's birthday!" B.C. shouted.

"And what should people get on their birthdays?" she asked.

"Cake! Birthday cake!" B.C. shouted it as he twirled around the Dalton kitchen. He dashed over to me and tugged on my sweatshirt so he could whisper in my ear. When I leaned over, he yelled, "Jen is making you a birthday cake!"

I was so touched, I couldn't say a word. Nobody had made me a birthday cake since I was seven years old. Dotty always brought one back from Hy-Klas. But my mom used to make a real cake herself. I can still picture my birthday cake with red icing and seven red candles and a tiny, black plastic horse on the top.

I remembered something else Mom made for my seventh birthday. For a whole week, I'd watched her paste strips of newspaper on top of a plaster mold. Slowly it took on the form of a big horse.

Two days before my birthday Mom painted the horse black with a white blaze to look like Orphan. The morning of my birthday she filled the paper mâche horse with candy and called it a *piñata*.

Ray and several other kids from church came for my party. We were supposed to hit the horse with a broom and knock out the candy. I got more and more anxious the closer we got to that part of the party. I didn't want anybody hitting the mini-Orphan with a broom.

When it was time for the piñata, instead of bringing out the broom, Mom had all the candy in a big bowl. She threw it in all directions over our yard. The other kids scrambled after candy, but I walked up to my mom, who somehow had read my mind.

"Scoop," she said, handing me a piece of candy she hadn't thrown, "hope you don't mind. I just couldn't see hitting that horse. Seemed wrong."

Jen had B.C. stirring with a wooden spoon, while she cracked eggs. She had the recipes right up in her head. Even Stephen seemed to get into the spirit of it after a while. He tore the bread into pieces for the stuffing, while I chopped celery and onions.

We must have worked like that for a half-hour or an hour even. From somewhere in the house, chimes sounded and a clock struck 10:00. It didn't seem possible.

"Only two hours left of your birthday, Scoop," Jen said. "I guess we better get your cake into the oven." With B.C. trailing close behind her, Jen carried over a rectangular, silver pan of would-be chocolate birthday cake.

"Careful, B.C.," Stephen called from his post by the turkey.

"You know," I said, wiping my onion tears with the back of my hand, "this really isn't such a bad birthday after all."

That's when everything went totally dark.

15

It wasn't just in the kitchen. The lights had gone off all over the house.

"Ah-h-h-h-h-H-H-H-H-H-H-H—H-H-H-!" B.C.'s scream started low as a hum and picked up volume until it was the only sound in the total blackness of the kitchen.

I couldn't see my own hand in front of my face. "B.C.!" I screamed. "Stop screaming!"

A light from a star popped through the black void outside the window. It was the only light and made me feel like I was standing outside under that lone star.

B.C.'s scream held steady as a Percheron plow horse in an Amish cornfield.

Somebody, probably Stephen, was flicking a light switch on and off, on and off, as if that would make the lights come back. "It's not the light switch," Jen said from somewhere to my right. "The electricity is off everywhere."

B.C.'s scream hadn't let up at all. I wondered how he could get that much air into those little lungs. Waving my arms around me so I wouldn't bump into anything, I groped my way to B.C. and put one arm around his shoulder.

"B.C.," I said in a calm voice, "don't be afraid. I'm here. And God's here, right? God's everywhere, so that means He's here too, right?"

"Stop flipping that switch, Stephen!" Jen ordered. "Go get us some candles."

"I don't know where any candles are," Stephen whined. *You* go get candles. How do we know somebody didn't cut our electricity lines on purpose? Maybe it's those convicts. Maybe they're hiding out there right now, just waiting—"

"Stop!" I cried.

But I was too late. B.C., who had slowed and lowered his mournful screaming, now started up louder and more scared than ever. "YIIIIIIIIIIIIIIIIIIIIIIII!"

Holding B.C. was like holding a tiny, frightened bird in my palm, feeling him tremble and knowing he was so scared that nothing I could say would help.

"Good job, Stephen!" Jen shouted. "Get out of here and get us candles!"

I remembered the candles B.C. had knocked over that afternoon. "On the mantel in the living room," I called. "There are some gold candles there."

"We can't use those candles," Stephen said.

"Get them!" Jen yelled.

A shuffling and grumbling came from Stephen's corner. Then I heard the sound of something falling over in the living room, followed by Stephen yelling a couple of words I was glad B.C. couldn't hear because he was still screaming.

"Scoop?" Jen asked, as sounds of her shuffling feet came closer to us.

"I'm here with B.C.," I said, his cry acting like a kind of lighthouse, only with sound instead of light guiding ships to shore.

"B.C.," Jen said, loud but calm, as if she didn't realize he was screaming. "I'm going to tell you a secret about Tommy, but I don't want you to let him know I told."

B.C. didn't stop screaming, but it softened to near normal voice level.

"Tommy Zucker, my rough, tough brother, is afraid of the dark," Jen said.

B.C.'s scream shut off like electricity. "Tommy?"

"Yes," Jen said, standing on the other side of B.C., her hand brushing my wrist as she put her arm around B.C.'s shoulder. "If Tommy were here right now, you know what?"

"What?" B.C. asked.

"He'd be a scaredy cat."

B.C. didn't speak, but at least he didn't scream again.

"B.C.," Jen said, "will you look out for

Scoop while I go find us some matches? Then we'll light some candles."

I felt B.C.'s head nod.

Jen shuffled away. Drawers opened, rustled, slammed shut. Drawer after drawer after drawer.

Footsteps came from the other side of the kitchen. Even knowing that it had to be Stephen, I couldn't help imagining those convicts, still in chains, creeping around the mansion.

Then Stephen broke the silence. "I've got the candles."

"Yes!" Jen shouted from the other side of the kitchen. "And I've got the matches! Okay. Let's all move slowly to the table."

I walked with B.C., a tiny step at a time. We bumped into something that felt like a table. "Jen?" I called, my hand reaching across the table. My fingers fell on something cold and clammy. "Yuk! What's that?" I jerked back my hand and shuddered.

"Over here, Scoop!" Jen answered. "You're probably at the butcher block."

She was right, and I'd just touched the giant dead turkey, the turkey we weren't going to get to eat now that the electricity was out. And no birthday cake either.

Chairs squeaked against the floor, and I guided B.C. toward the sound. I felt the back of a chair. "Here, B.C.," I said, pressing down on his shoulder. "Sit here."

I moved around until my leg hit another chair, and I backed onto it.

"Hey! Get off!" Stephen cried.

I bounced up off his lap and circled the table to the next chair, an empty one this time.

A spark lit the room for a second, like a tiny flash bulb, then disappeared.

"Wait," Jen muttered. "I'll get it."

"Don't waste matches," Stephen said. Jen ignored him and struck another match. This time it stayed lit, showing Jen's hand and her face in flickering, golden light. "Hurry! Get the candles over here."

Stephen set both candles in the center of table. Jen lit one, then used it to light the second candle. "There."

We could see. Almost instantly the whole kitchen turned from a nightmare into a beautiful, softly lit room.

"And Jesus said, 'I am the Light of the World,'" Jen said, separating the candles to give us a broader light. One of them made a *ping* as it bumped into the pan of unbaked cake.

Across from me at the table, B.C. sat perfectly still. I could see the tear stains on his cheeks and his runny nose. But he looked angelic in the dancing candlelight. I ached inside for everything that might ever go wrong in his life.

"These are pretty candles," B.C. said. He was right. I'd never seen gold candles with jewels set right into them. The candleholders wound around like brass grapevines.

"They ought to be," Stephen said. "Mother had to go all the way to Florence, Italy, to get them. They're not supposed to be burned."

I expected Jen to say something clever to that, but she didn't. She wasn't paying any attention to us. Her fingers drummed on the table, and I heard her toe tapping nervously. "I need some water," she said.

Had all of this made her *need* her stupid drugs? Was that it?

"Stay there, Jen," I said, scooting back my chair. "I'll get you a glass of water."

The candles gave me enough light to find a glass and fill it for Jen. I sat it in front of her, daring her to think up another excuse, another way to get to her precious pills.

She took the water without a thanks and didn't take a sip.

"What about birthday cake?" B.C. asked. "I thought Scoop was going to get a cake. You said she would, Jen. You said." B.C. was tottering on the edge of mania. I could hear it in his voice.

"Hey, B.C.," I said softly. I pulled over the rectangular tin of cake batter. "You know how your favorite part of the cake is licking the bowl? Well, I don't think Dotty would mind—just this once—if we tested the batter." I dipped my index finger into the cake batter and licked.

"Mmmmm. Try it."

"Gross!" Stephen said. "That's disgusting."

B.C. stuck his whole hand in the batter.

While B.C. licked the batter off his hand, Jen and Stephen and I discussed what our next move should be. We were stuck in the house until morning—that much was for sure. And morning wasn't that far off. We couldn't eat turkey or cake, but we gathered what we could from the sterile Dalton kitchen. While we talked, we munched on olives and ate some of the bread we hadn't torn up for stuffing.

Jen seemed in a hurry to get our discussion over with. "So that's it then. Stephen can get us blankets. And we need to get a fire going in the fireplace. I guess we're done here."

"What about the horses?" I asked. "Stephen, your boarded horses don't have winter coats like ours do. Those stable blankets you make them wear won't do them much good in the cold. And what about that mare in the last stall? When is she due? She looks really close, if you ask me."

"I don't know," Stephen said. "We pay the night groom to watch for the foals. And the day grooms take care of everything else."

"Okay, then," Jen said, scooting her chair back, like she couldn't wait to get away.

I knew what she wanted. She wanted her pills. I could see it in her eyes. And I wasn't going to let it happen. Right now was as good a time as any for my friend to kick her drug habit.

I grabbed one of the candles before Jen could. "Wait just a minute, will you? I-I need to go to the bathroom. Wait here. I'll be fast."

I strode out of the kitchen, leaving them to share the other candle. The flame on mine tipped back as I walked, and I cupped my hand around it, afraid it would go out.

With the candle in front of me, I circled the living room to the bay window sill ... and Jen's coat. Maybe if she could get through one night without her drugs, she could beat the habit. I had to try. Her coat was right where I'd left it.

From the kitchen came a scraping sound, someone getting up. I felt in one of the coat pockets, but I couldn't get at the pills with only one hand. Setting the candle down on the sill, I picked up Jen's coat. I tried one pocket. Then another. Where were they?

Behind me, footsteps sounded. A soft thud came from the living room, as if somebody had bumped into something. I had to hurry. Where were those pills?

The inside pocket! Suddenly I remembered. I felt inside, pushing my hand all the way down. There. The rumpled, cold, aluminum foil packet was still there. My fingers closed around the foil.

A hand on my arm swung me around. Jen Zucker stood over me. "What on earth do you think you're doing?"

16

I stared at the face washed in candlelight and shadows. It didn't even look like Jen. Her eyes were black slits, and the light made her blond hair look black.

"Answer me!" she shouted. "What are you trying to do? And give me my coat!" She jerked the coat out of my hands. The packet of pills flew to the floor.

We both bent down and scrambled for the foil packet. Jen came up with it. "I knew it!" she yelled. "You have no business going through my things!" I couldn't tell if the tremor in her voice came from outrage or shame. She turned her back on me.

"Jen, please," I pleaded. "Let me help. Tell me what it is. Tell me what's wrong."

She wheeled back around. "Travis said something to you, didn't he? Of course! He had no right."

"Travis is worried about you, Jen," I said. "And so am I."

"You two should mind your own business!"

She started off, and I grabbed her arm. "What's in that packet, Jen? Tell me! You've got pills in there, don't you? Don't lie to me."

Jen jerked her arm away so hard, my whole arm felt the pain of my bite wound. "Leave—me—alone." She pronounced each word distinctly, with such force that her words sent a shiver through me.

"What is it?" B.C. looked at us with big, sad eyes. I hadn't heard him walk up. "Please don't fight. I don't like it when you fight."

I put one hand on top of B.C.'s head and scruffed his hair. Static electricity made his hair stick to my hand. When I lifted my hand, tiny white sparks flew up.

Calmly I said, "Jen, I know what's going on. I want to help."

"You don't have the slightest idea what's going on," she said. She walked away, shaking her head.

Candlelight made everything look like it was under water. It felt like Jen was swimming away, caught in some kind of dangerous undertow. I hadn't helped her. If anything, I'd made it so she'd never trust me. No way was she going to talk to me now.

Stephen joined B.C. and me with our candle, while Jen returned to the kitchen table. When I looked in, I saw her bent over her journal, writing so fast I could hear the pen scratch.

"I'm freezing!" Stephen complained.

"Then I guess we better make a fire," I said. "Let's get some wood in."

"Come on, B.C.," Stephen said. "There's a wood box out back."

It took the better part of an hour. None of us really knew what we were doing, but finally we had a fire in the fireplace. The Daltons had a special gas line feeding into the fireplace, so it only took one try to light it.

"Did you open the flue?" Jen called out from the kitchen.

We stared stupidly at each other. Gray smoke puffed back at us from the chimney. Stephen shoved a metal pipe that stuck out on one side of the fireplace. It clanked, and all the smoke was sucked up the chimney. "Of course we opened the flue!" Stephen yelled back.

B.C. laughed. So did I. So did Stephen.

Jen, carrying her candle, walked down the hall without even glancing our way. In a minute, she came back with her arms full of candles.

Our fire put out plenty of light and heat as long we stayed close. The flames swayed back and forth as wind from the chimney hit them. Outside, something howled, probably the wind. But the sound lasted long. I felt B.C. tense up and heard him begin his little manic noises between his teeth: chi-chi-chi-chi.

I had to distract him. "Stephen," I said pleasantly, like we were on a picnic, "would you please bring us a couple of blankets to sit on?"

He started to protest, but I caught his eye. *Please, God,* I prayed, *make Stephen understand. I need help with B.C.*

"Sure," Stephen said, heading off somewhere down the long hall.

I sat down, and tried to pull B.C. gently beside me, but his whole body felt stiff and he kept making the chattering noises, staring at the fire. "I think I feel like telling a story, B.C. What do you think?"

Somewhere in the house the clock struck midnight. B.C. jumped at the first gong, then shook for the other 11. Stephen got back with an armful of quilts and spread one out in front of the fire. I scooted over onto it. Stephen sat down on the edge and poked at the logs in the fire. The heat of it warmed my cheek.

"Come on, B.C. I'll tell you a horse story," I offered. "How about an Orphan story?"

"Orphan," Stephen said. "That's such a dumb name for a horse. Now *Champion,* there's a name for you. But *Orphan?* Why would you ever name her that?" Normally, those would have been fighting words coming from Stephen Dalton. But this time it sounded different, not mean at all. It was almost like he was in on my secret attempt to distract my brother.

Whether Stephen knew what he was doing, it worked. B.C. stopped chattering. He turned his head, and the flames splashed shadows on his cheek. "Champion's a dumb name for a horse. Orphan's a great name for a horse!"

"You think so?" Stephen asked.

B.C. nodded. This time when I pulled his hand, he let himself be pulled onto my lap.

"And *you* should think Orphan is a great name too, Stephen," I said, "because *you* named her."

"I did not," he said, sounding too much like the old Stephen. Had I imagined the other one?

"You did," I said. "We were three years old. My parents had just adopted me. They brought me over to Grandad's barn to meet him. And there was this tiny, black foal, just born."

"And her mother died," B.C. said, repeating the story I must have told him a hundred times. "And nobody could get the foal to drink out of the bottle, except Scoop."

"That's right, B.C.," I said. "Then came the Daltons. Stephen's dad brought little *Stevie* to Grandad's to meet me. I was feeding the bottle to Orphan and stroking her neck. Then I saw this little boy all dressed up in a suit and tie, his bright red hair slicked down like Sundays."

"That was *you, Stee*-ven!" B.C. shouted.

"I don't remember any of this," Stephen said, like he thought we were just making it up.

But we weren't.

"And this little kid the same age as me stuck out his finger and pointed right at me and screamed, *Orphan! Orphan!*"

B.C. stuck out his finger at Stephen and repeated, "Orphan! Orphan!"

"Yep," I continued. "And Stephen meant to call *me* that, because I *was* an orphan. But I thought he was calling the foal *Orphan*. So I hugged that black foal and said, 'Orphan.' And it was the very first word I'd spoken, or at least that my folks had heard me speak. 'Orphan!' I said. And that's been her wonderful, beautiful name every since."

"No way!" Stephen said, but he was trying not to laugh. "That never happened."

"Did too!" B.C. protested, just like he'd been there and seen it with his own eyes.

Stephen broke out his secret stash of candy bars. I downed a Milky Way in three bites. While B.C. and Stephen stuffed their mouths beside the fire, I peeked into the kitchen. Jen didn't look up from her journal, not even when I cleared my throat.

She was never going to open up to me—especially not after I'd tried to get her precious pills from her. If only I could see what she was writing. Then I'd know what she was thinking. Maybe she'd even written in there the kinds of drugs she'd been messing with, and for how long. That's the kind of information I wanted to be able to give Travis.

Watching Jen scribble in her journal, I made up my mind. Before this night was over I'd get that information for Travis—one way or another.

A thump sounded as if someone upstairs were knocking on the ceiling. Jen looked up from her journal. Then a *bang, bang, bamm* erupted, followed by a loud clatter.

"Help!" This time it was Stephen screaming. "Oh no! They're here!"

I ran in to B.C., who seemed frozen to the fireside blanket. Steven was standing, staring at the ceiling. It did sound like we were being attacked. Jen hobbled in from the kitchen.

Again crashing and banging clattered over our heads.

We screamed and hit the floor, piling on top of one another. I imagined dozens of escaped felons bearing down on us.

"What is it?" Jen whispered, her voice muffled.

I looked up and saw huge shadows covering the ceiling. They swooped our way, with hideous cries of *eee-eee-eee-eee-eee!* I threw a quilt over our heads, and we huddled together in the dark ... waiting ... and wondering. Who or what was attacking?

17

It's the prisoners! The jailbirds! The convicts!"
Stephen whispered. His face was so close to
mine I could smell his chocolate breath and feel
his spit.

"It's not convicts," Jen whispered back from
somewhere on the other side of B.C. "Not
unless they learned how to fly in prison."

"So what is it?" I whispered.

"I'm scared," B.C. said, crying softly.

"I don't know what it is," Jen said, "but I'm
going to find out." I felt Jen struggling to her
feet. She threw off her end of the quilt like a
cloak. "I'm not afraid of you!" she shouted.

"Jen, don't!" I cried, trying to pull her back
to the safety of our tent. I wondered if the drugs
had turned her bold, brazen, daring. I'd
promised Travis I'd look out for her.

"Stay here, B.C.," I said, getting to my feet.
I crept out from under the quilt and saw Jen
standing bravely in the center of the living room.
Flames jumped inside the fireplace, casting dancing shadows around the living room.

I took a step toward Jen, then stopped when I heard the eerie, squeaking cry again, like a ghost weeping. All at once a winged creature descended, followed by two more.

"Bats! It's a bat attack!" Jen shouted.

The bats circled the living room, swooping low, the big one in the lead.

"Bats?" Stephen appeared by my side. "Did she say bats?"

They swooped straight at us. We screamed and ducked as they flew over and disappeared down the hall.

"B.C.!" Stephen yelled. "Did you go in our attic? That's the only way they could get in."

B.C. stuck his head out of the quilt. "You mean a little door to a little room way up high?"

Now every shadow, every flicker of firelight looked like a bat.

"You brought those bats out of hibernation!" Stephen screamed.

"Don't yell at him," I shouted. *"You're* the one living in a bat cave!"

"I'm getting the shotgun," Stephen announced.

I grabbed his sleeve. "Don't you dare! No way I'm being in the same house with a shotgun ... and *you!*"

He tried to pull away, but I wouldn't let go. I didn't even like knowing there was a gun in the house. I'd rather have a house full of bats.

"Oh, all right," Stephen said. "I'll go get a bat."

"No!" B.C. cried. "We already have bats!"

"A baseball bat," Stephen explained. "I'll get a baseball bat to clobber the bat bats."

"Nobody is going to hurt those bats," Jen said. "Bats are our friends."

"Yeah right," Stephen headed for the hall closet.

"I mean it, Stephen." And you could tell Jen did mean it. "Bats are the most endangered land mammals in North America. We need bats."

"Maybe *you* need bats, Wonder Woman," Stephen muttered. *"I* do not."

"They suck your blood," B.C. said.

"They do not suck your blood, B.C.," Jen explained. "But they do eat mosquitoes, and mosquitoes suck your blood. Plus, bats protect crops by eating beetles, moths, and leaf-hoppers—to say nothing of what bat droppings do!"

"Please spare us the bat-dropping speech," Stephen pleaded. "I give up. No gun. No *ball* bat. So what are we supposed to do with them, bake another cake?"

"Just catch them, gently, and turn them loose outside. And close the attic door," Jen added.

The bats swooped above us, and we ducked again.

"They're going upstairs!" Jen cried. "After

them! When they fly into a room, close the door. They'll be easier to trap in a smaller space."

We raced for the stairs, and Stephen was so polite he let me go up first. Jen watched from the bottom of the stairs. I'd almost forgotten about her sore ankle.

The biggest bat rammed one of the doors at the top of the stairs. The door was slightly open anyway, and the bat slid in easily. The other bats flew in after it.

I grabbed the doorknob and pulled the door shut, trapping all three bats inside. "Got it!" I yelled. "All three of them!" I held the door shut with all my might, as if they might try to pull it open.

B.C. put his hands on top of mine as I clutched the doorknob. "We got 'em!" he shouted. "Neh-neh neh-neh neh-neh nch neh—Batman!" he sang.

"Well done, Robin," I said.

"Wait a minute." Stephen stood behind us staring at the bat room. "That's my bedroom!"

"Don't worry," I said. "You're throwing the bats outside anyway, right?"

"Me?" Stephen asked. "I can't get them by myself, Scoop."

"Hey!" From the bottom of the stairs, Jen threw something up at us. "Use these!"

I picked up a catcher's mask, a pair of down mittens, and a stocking cap. Stephen grabbed the catcher's mitt and a fielder's glove, plus his bike helmet. We put on our armor.

"Stand back, B.C.," I said solemnly, facing the bat room, imagining the three bats lined up like fighter pilots, like stealth bombers, waiting for their target. I glanced at Stephen. He looked pretty funny in his get-up.

He glanced over at me and nodded.

I nodded back.

"You first," he said.

"*You* first," I said.

We stood staring at the white wood door, the door to battle, the door to bats. I heard Stephen's heavy breathing over my own. Seconds passed. Minutes.

I turned to Stephen. He turned to me. And at the same instant, we took off our helmets and catcher's mask, threw down our gloves and mittens, and stepped away from the door.

"I guess it wouldn't be so bad to wait until daylight," I said.

"I guess I could let them use my room for one night," Stephen said.

We walked past B.C., down the stairs, past Jen, and back to the living room.

Jen limped quietly up to us and put a hand on Stephen's and my shoulders. "Brave lads. Well done, heroes. Now, Batmen, let's just hope we don't get *robins.*"

L et's try to get some sleep," I suggested.
"I don't have my pajamas!" B.C. cried. "I
need my pajamas."

I'd been in the same clothes for almost 24
hours. They'd gotten wet, dried, gotten wet
again, and dried. "I could sure use a night-
gown," I said.

"Hey," Stephen said, "my mother is the only
one in this house who has nightgowns."

"I'm very glad to hear it, Stephen," I said.

He refused to invade his parents' bedroom
to get us something to sleep in. So Jen did. She
came out a minute later with her arms full of candles, a fancy kerosene lantern, and two thick,
fluffy gowns that might have been robes.

"That's the biggest bedroom I've ever
seen," she said. "And they have their own swimming pool or hot tub in there. Did you know
that?"

"Nope," I said, not surprised though. We
headed for one of the downstairs bathrooms that
was bigger than our living room. I couldn't

remember the last time I'd been invited to the Dalton house, but it had been years ago. I had an idea where some things were—the kitchen, the bathrooms. But everything must have been remodeled with all new furniture.

I put on the turquoise robe-nightgown that had to be the softest thing I'd ever had next to my skin. B.C. had to make do with a pajama top that belonged to Stephen's dad because Stephen refused to go into his bat room.

B.C. and I stretched out in front of the warm fireplace, and he was out and snoring instantly. Stephen leaned back in the fireside recliner and piled on covers. In another minute, he was snoring like B.C., a duet of snores that kept me awake.

For a while Jen read or wrote in the kitchen by the light of the kerosene lantern. Then she settled down on the couch with two extra blankets and a pile of books she'd scrounged from the Dalton library.

Stephen's snores grew louder. From time to time he'd mumble something in his sleep, like, "No, no, I didn't do it!"

It was no use trying to sleep. Finally I gave up and ambled to the bay window to see if the snow had let up. A hazy moon made the snow look like a glittering sea of white caps. Two bright stars blinked.

Father, I prayed, looking at the night beauty

God had created in the middle of this frightening storm. *I'm so afraid of everything, and I can't seem to do anything to make it better. What's going to happen to Jen? She doesn't trust me any more than her horse does. And Dotty? What if she decides to just stay in Cinnamon Lake forever? I could never leave Horsefeathers.*

I tried to remember the verse we'd memorized in youth group that fall—something about being afraid. Then I got it—just like it happens sometimes when I pray. I remembered a verse from Psalm 34:

I sought the LORD, and He answered me; He delivered me from all my fears. ... This poor man called, and the LORD heard him; He saved him out of all his troubles. The angel of the LORD encamps around those who fear Him, and He delivers them (Psalm 34:4, 6–7).

I couldn't remember the middle part, but just feeling the words about being delivered from fear seemed to help. I tried to picture an angel camped around us, but all I could bring to mind were the snow angels I'd made with Orphan.

One minute I looked toward the couch, and Jen was reading. The next minute she was asleep, a book tented over her face.

I wandered into the kitchen for a drink. The kerosene lamp burned with a slow, dancing flame that was enough for me to see what I was doing.

I sat at the kitchen table to drink my water by kerosene lantern. There next to the light was a brown, hard-backed book—Jen's journal.

Jen was asleep, and I had her journal. I picked it up and felt the fat book, filled with Jen's thoughts I couldn't break into. But I could break into this book. All it would take was to open the pages and read. In my hands were the answers to whatever had Jen so worried she'd turned to drugs instead of turning to her friends, her family, or to God. I'd told Travis I'd try to get answers for him. Here were answers.

Taking a deep breath, I prayed, *God, please forgive me for what I'm about to do*.

I shifted the journal to my left palm and got ready to turn pages with my right index finger.

But I couldn't. How could I do something that I knew ahead of time would require God's forgiveness? I asked God to show me a better way to help Jen, one that didn't require snooping through Jen's journal. Carefully, I set down the journal and rested my elbows on the table, my head in my hands.

"Scoop?"

I jerked my head up and saw Jen Zucker standing in the entry of the kitchen.

"Horsefeathers! Jen?" I exclaimed. "I thought you were—. This isn't what you think. I didn't read your journal. Honest I didn't!"

"I know," she said. "I was watching you."

She limped, just slightly, to the table and sat across from me. "Thanks for not reading my journal."

"I wanted to, Jen," I admitted. "I'm scared. Scared for you, scared of everything."

Jen picked up her journal. "I know," she replied. "Me too."

I waited, praying, afraid to say the wrong thing again.

Jen opened to a page in her journal and without explanation began reading to me:

September 10: I'm tired. I'm so completely tired. And I'm sick and tired of feeling sick and tired. What is going on with me? This isn't normal, not for me it isn't.

Jen stopped, and I felt a fear begin to bubble inside of me. September 10 was two and a half months ago.

She turned a couple of pages and read on: *The twins and triplets and I have doctor's appointments on Friday, just for regular check-ups. I'm thinking about telling the doctor how rotten I've been feeling.*

Saturday: What a journey to the doctor's! That poor, receptionist! I could see the dread in her eyes when we walked into the waiting room. I think we lived up to her expectations—and we didn't even have Tommy with us!

I asked Dr. Lyle what he thought about my being so tired all the time. Doc says what I've got is just womanly tiredness and I should be sure I'm getting good rest and exercise and eating right.

More pages turned, their soft rustle the only noise in the kitchen. Jen backed up a page. "You'll like this one," she said, glancing up at me. Her face shone with the moving kerosene light. *"Travis got himself a horse today, a gorgeous Appaloosa gelding, sweet-natured and a good ride. He renamed the horse Angel, and I've never seen him so excited. We owe it all to Scoop—who, by the way, is the world's best horse whisperer."*

"Horsefeathers, Jen," I said. "I didn't know you thought that."

Jen kept her gaze on her journal and continued reading as if she hadn't heard what I said. *"Something is definitely wrong with me, and it isn't just womanly tiredness. Not to be gross or anything, but after I use the bathroom, I can see that my urine is so yellow it looks gold. Tonight it looked brown. I'm going to ask Mom to make me a doctor's appointment."*

I wished I were smarter, that I could figure out what was wrong with Jen by what she was reading from her journal. But I still had no idea. I wanted her to skip to the end where she found out. Was that why she was taking drugs? Did she do it to escape whatever was wrong with her? I dug my fingernails into my palms to keep from erupting in a million questions that might make Jen stop talking again.

Sick again! I hate missing school, falling behind. I'm never sick this often. At the clinic the doctors acted like I was making up my symptoms to get attention or something. Doc should know me better than that.

In the next room, the squeaky sound of Steven's recliner footstool was followed by some unintelligible gibberish. Then the house fell silent again, except for the howl of the wind, and my heart beating.

Jen turned the page. *The tests came back. I've got blood in my urine and protein too. Doc Lyle told Mom that the test might be a fluke. Maybe I have an infection or something like that. I asked the startled receptionist to mail me a copy of the report. She refused until I convinced her it was my information in the first place.*

Jen skipped over a bunch of journal entries. *I made Mom and Dad promise not to say anything to Travis and the kids. A copy of the lab reports arrived yesterday. I spent hours on the Internet, reading everything I could find about my symptoms—and what I can expect from now on.*

"Is that why you've been on the computers in the school library so much?" I asked. "I thought you were doing research for a paper."

"I've read hundreds of articles on it, Scoop," Jen said. "I've studied hospital web sites, e-mailed questions and gotten specific answers. I've read the studies on experimental medicines.

I've probably read more about it than most doctors."

"About *what*, Jen? What are you talking about?" I couldn't take it in. There were the drugs. What about those? And the tiredness. I couldn't put it together. "What is wrong with you?" I demanded.

Jen put down her journal and looked me squarely in the eyes. "I think I'm going to die."

19

Jen's words seemed to bounce around the shadowy kitchen: *I think I'm going to die. I think I'm going to die.*

Tears burned in my chest and my throat. I stared at her over the lantern. Grandad had died, and it was awful, but he was old. He'd lived his life. Jen hadn't. "Don't say that," I said weakly.

"The disease is called nephritis. It's a kidney disease, and both of my kidneys are giving out. That's why I'm so tired all the time. We've been back to the clinic for all kinds of tests. Doc Lyle confirmed it."

"So what can they do to cure you?" I asked.

"Not much," she answered. "Kidney damage can't be *cured*. What's gone is gone, and I won't get it back. My kidneys aren't doing a good job cleaning my blood. That's why I don't have a good immunity to colds and flu."

"There *has* to be something they can do!" I insisted.

"There's a blood pressure medicine that takes some of the work off the kidneys. I've been taking that for a week. But it makes me dizzy. So I take a couple of things for nausea. But they make me sleepy, so—"

"Pills?" I asked, light dawning on me as if someone had drawn back curtains from my brain. "Those pills in your pockets?"

"Yeah," Jen said. "Sorry about that. I just didn't want anybody to know—not even Travis. Mom and Dad promised they wouldn't tell the kids until I was ready."

"Jen!" I exclaimed, slapping my hand on the table so hard the lantern shook, sending the shadows scattering on the walls. "I thought you were on drugs!"

"What?" she asked, wrinkling her tiny, China-doll nose.

"Drugs!" I repeated, flipping back and forth from feeling relieved to feeling worse. "I thought you were a drug addict."

We laughed, first just soft chuckles. But it felt so good, I laughed harder. Then Jen laughed, and I laughed at her laughing.

Then as suddenly as it had started, our laughter faded and we sat still and silent across from each other, lost in our thoughts.

"What about getting an artificial kidney—like an artificial heart?" I asked.

Jen shook her head. "There isn't such a thing for kidneys."

"Then what about a kidney transplant? You

can have one of mine," I offered. "We've got two, right?"

Jen grinned. "Thanks, Scoop," she said. "I refuse to have a transplant."

"But wouldn't it help you? Jen, you can't refuse."

"That's one of the reasons I won't let Mom tell Travis. Kidney transplants are huge operations, Scoop. The idea of one terrifies me. I won't do it. And for it to work, Doc says we'd need a biological donor. That means Travis or Tommy probably. Even if I weren't too scared to have the operation, I'd be too scared something would happen to my brother and it would be my fault."

"But you *have* to, right? To save your life?"

Jen shook her head no, as if there would be no changing her mind. "I won't do it. Not to me. And not to Travis or Tommy."

"Your mother will make you do it," I insisted. Mrs. Zucker loves her children so much, you can almost see them in her eyes when you look deep. There was no way she would stand by and watch her daughter die.

"Mom wants to believe that I won't get bad enough to need a transplant, Scoop. I'm going to let her believe she's right."

"Maybe she *is* right," I said, hoping, praying she was.

"She's not. Doc gave me three warning signs to look out for. When they show up, it means

I'm in the end stages of renal failure."

I knew it before she got the words out. She was there.

"You have to tell!" I said, crying. "Travis deserves to know. He'll want to help, Jen. I know he will."

Jen shook her head again. "I won't do it. I get so scared every time I have to go into that hospital to get blood drawn. No way could I make it through a transplant operation."

"Why are you yelling?" B.C.'s tiny voice reminded me of when he was a baby. He stood in the doorway, the moonlight shining a stripe across him, like a banner of honor. He rubbed his eyes with his fists. "I woke up and you weren't there! And I was scared. And I didn't know where I was or where you were or Dotty. What if Dotty's stuck in a ditch? What if nobody ever comes for us." His voice rose with every word until he was screaming and waving his arms in the air, as if he were brushing off bees. "I'm afraid!" he screamed. "I'm afraid!"

I felt scared for B.C., scared for Jen, scared for all of us. I ran over and picked up my brother like I used to do when he was a baby. "It's okay, B.C.," I said, sniffing. "We're all scared."

B.C. reached up with one hand and touched the tears on my cheeks. His hand felt like ice.

"Jen, come on back by the fire," I said, carrying B.C. through the living room.

The fire had burned down to ashes. "We need kindling," I said, setting B.C. down. "And more logs."

Jen followed us to the woodbox, with only a slight limp. All the while Stephen kept snoring from his recliner.

The woodbox was empty. I didn't know where to find wood under all that snow. But I couldn't let us freeze to death. We walked back to the living room. The Daltons had more furniture in that one room than we had in our whole house. My gaze landed on a wooden chair sitting all by itself in the corner. What would one chair matter in a room full of them?

"Stephen?" I called.

"Honk-pshhhh." His answer was a louder snore.

I shook his arm gently. "Stephen! We need firewood!"

"Huh?" he said, his beady eyes flying open. "Okay." He rolled back over and pulled up the covers.

I looked around at B.C., who shrugged.

"Stephen!" I yelled in his ear. "Is it okay if we break up that chair for firewood? And maybe those two or three over there by the door?" I pointed to the chairs arranged in a semi-circle by the front door.

"Yeah, good idea," Stephen said, not rolling over or opening his eyes.

"Are you sure?" I asked. "Your parents won't mind?"

"That's good," Stephen answered, and he picked up his snoring where he'd left off.

Jen and B.C. helped me break up the chairs and toss them into the fireplace. They caught fast, and flames jumped to life and warmth. We huddled by the fire, while Stephen kept up a steady snore.

"How come I get so a-scared of everything?" B.C. asked. He was nestled between Jen and me, sticking to us like peanut butter in a sandwich. "You don't get a-scared like me."

"Everybody gets scared, B.C.," I said. I thought about all the things I'd been afraid of in the last month. "Since way back Halloween night, when those bales were on fire at Horsefeathers, I've been afraid of losing everything."

Jen reached back and pulled down the footstool of Stephen's recliner. He flipped up and almost fell over the arm of the chair. "What— why did you do that?" he whined.

"Because I want an answer, Stephen," Jen said.

"Leave me alone," he groaned.

"Not until I get a straight answer. Sit up so we can see your face."

Grumbling and moaning, Stephen sat all the way up in the chair. He pulled the blanket around him like a shawl. "All right. Are you satisfied? Ask your stupid question so I can get back to sleep."

"I want to know if you set fire to the hay at Horsefeathers on Halloween. And if you lie about it, you'll be really sorry." You could tell Jen had grown up in a big family. She knew how to boss.

"I didn't do it," Stephen said. "Honest! I wasn't even there."

I turned and studied his face. I would probably never believe a word that came out of his mouth, but Stephen Dalton has a face that doesn't lie. He was telling the truth.

Jen must have seen it too. "All right. Go back to sleep."

I'd probably never know who really set the fire at Horsefeathers—most likely, some kids carried away with trick-or-treating, like the fire-fighters had told us. But it didn't make the fear go away. It was like a thousand bad things were out there and could happen at any moment. And I'd never even know where they came from.

"It's different to be afraid about Horsefeathers catching fire, or worrying about Orphan and the horses," B.C. said, his gaze fixed on the burning chair leg. "But you and Jen weren't afraid when the lights went out. And you were brave when the bats attacked."

"I was scared, B.C.," I said. "And I'm scared of other things too—like for Dotty." I stopped myself before I unloaded too much on him again. I changed the subject fast. "And you know how usually I can get just about any horse to trust me? Well somehow, Cheyenne can tell I'm scared. She won't relax with me. I can't get her to trust me again."

B.C. turned to Jen. "Is Tommy really afraid of the dark?"

"Yes," Jen answered softly.

"Are you ever afraid, Jen?" he asked.

Jen was quiet, and B.C. waited without interrupting or asking another question. Finally she said, "I'm afraid of dying."

I thought her answer might make B.C. go off into one of his anxiety fits or something. Instead he reached up and put his hand on Jen's shoulder. "You know what Dotty told me about dying?" he asked. "She said that maybe before we were born, when we were in our mamas' tummies waiting to come out, that maybe we were scared to leave. Maybe we thought that little tiny space inside our moms was all there was, so whatever was outside, it had to be scary." B.C. was quiet for a minute.

"But that was just a tiny bit of the world," he went on. "And the really good stuff—like chocolate pudding and bottle caps—that was all waiting for us out here. So we were kind of silly to think that where we were was all there was.

"Dotty said that's like being afraid of dying.

She says Jesus wouldn't have died for our sins like that on a cross just to be raised up so we could join Him in a scary place. He did all that so we could be forgiven and go to heaven. And in heaven, He's making mansions bigger than the Dalton's mansion. So that's a mighty fine place to be born to when we die."

Tears were trickling down my chin. I'd been there when Dotty had said those things. It was right after Grandad died. I couldn't believe my brother had understood it all. None of us would ever know what all went on inside B.C.'s head. When Pastor Dan baptized B.C., he'd talked about the comfort of eternal life that was God's gift. Until this moment, I never knew how much my own Baptism meant to me. God had given me the gift of faith and the reality of life with Him forever.

Stephen coughed. We turned to look at him, and I saw that he was wide awake, listening.

Jen said, "Come on, Stephen. Tell us. What are *you* afraid of?"

Stephen didn't answer. "What's—what's that in the fire?" he asked. "It looks like—"

"Please, *Stee*-ven," B.C. coaxed. "Isn't there nothing you're afraid of?"

Finally Stephen answered, spitting out one disgusting word: "Bats."

20

It seemed like I'd just dozed off when the phone woke me. The fire had completely burned out, and bright sunlight flooded the room. But it wasn't my little bedroom. An unfamiliar Lysol smell confused me. This wasn't the musty smell I usually woke up to.

Then it came back to me. I'd spent the night at the Dalton mansion. I crawled over B.C. to get to the phone. "Hello?" My voice sounded groggy and hoarse.

"Scoop? Oh, Scoop, Honey? Is that you? You ain't sick? Is B.C. okay? He ain't too scared, is he?" Dotty's voice woke me up like an alarm clock. It felt so good to have her there on the other end of the line.

"Dotty? Are *you* okay? Travis said you were stuck in Cinnamon Lake." *Please, God. Please don't let her want to stay there.*

"Well, I was," Dotty said. A woman's voice in the background said, "Hey Scoop! Happy Thanksgiving!" Then two other sharp voices hollered too: "Hi Scoop!" "Hey Sugar! Happy Turkey Day!"

"Dotty?" I asked her. "Who are those people?" I'd forgotten all about Thanksgiving.

"Why that's Rosa, and Adele, and An-gel-ique," she said, pronouncing the last name as if she'd had practice lessons on it. "Hey Dot!" one of them yelled. "You gonna eat your sausage?"

"Dotty?" I asked. "Where are you?"

"Thank you, Sheriff," Dotty said.

"Sheriff?" I pictured Dotty in a gray and white striped uniform, too tight around the middle. "Are you ... ? You're not ... in jail!"

"Well, yes I am," she said. "And I've met me the nicest folks here. Lord, thank You for Your surprises. I didn't listen to nobody and tried to drive home to you and B.C."

"You did?" I said. "You wanted to come home?"

"Like the foolish ol' woman that I am," she said. "I ain't got no further than a few miles in two hours. And this nice sheriff, he rescued me. I drove the car into a ditch. Did I say that? Anyway, it's fixed now, I reckon. So the only bed in town was right here in the hoosegow."

"The what?"

"The slammer!" shouted one of Dotty's new friends. "The joint!" said another, cackling.

"Sheriff says the roads had oughta be better by the afternoon, so I reckon I'll be there by nightfall. Can I talk at B.C.?"

"I'm glad you're coming home, Dotty," I

said. I nudged B.C. "Dotty's on the phone," I whispered.

That's all it took. "Dotty!" B.C. screamed.

Thanks, Lord, I said. *Two fears down.* Jen wasn't on drugs, and Dotty was coming home. *Now if we can just get Jen and Cheyenne to trust us,* I told God, almost feeling like Dotty as I talked things over with Him. *Please make Jen willing to do whatever she needs to do.*

Jen wasn't by the fire. She came in from the hall, all dressed. "The bats aren't there," she announced.

"Bats?" Stephen jerked awake in his recliner. His head rotated as he prepared for another attack.

"I think the bats must have *batted* their way back into your attic," Jen said. "Unless they're lying in wait for you, Stephen."

"Stephen," I said, gathering up my clothes, "I don't think your grooms can make it in this morning. You better get dressed. I'll help you with chores. Are you sure you don't know when that mare is supposed to have her foal. I still say she looks close."

"She's not. The night groom knows when she's due," Stephen muttered.

I found everything except one boot. "We may need to carry water from the house." I peered under the couch and found my other boot.

"That's really not my job," Stephen said, turning over and pulling up the covers.

I yanked the blankets off him. "It's your job this morning. Get up!"

When I came out of the bathroom, where I'd dressed, washed up, and brushed my teeth with toothpaste and my finger, Stephen was on the phone.

"Yes, Dad," Stephen whined. "They're all three still here. ... I don't know. I'll ask her."

Stephen covered the phone and shouted to Jen, "Is your ankle better?"

"It's better, but it still hurts to walk on it," Jen answered. She was setting bread and butter and jam out on the table in the kitchen. The jams were weird flavors like boysenberry and crabapple.

Stephen repeated Jen's answer into the phone. He listened. "Just a minute. I'll ask." Covering the mouthpiece again, he shouted, "Jen, were you on Dalton property when you fell? They said they'd forget about the broken stuff in the house if you forget where you hurt your ankle."

I ate two pieces of bread and drank a big glass of water. "Send Stephen out to the stable as soon as he's off the phone, okay, Jen?" I said, scooting back from the table.

B.C. was still eating when I finished bundling myself up for chores. "I'm almost done, Scoop," he shouted out to me. "I'll help."

"Thanks, B.C.," I called back to him as I opened the front door. "Take your time."

Outside the snow came down in tiny flakes that carried morning light on them. I squinted at the smooth, white blanket on the ground, brighter than silver. Trees carried the weight of it, their branches bending down to touch the drifts, bowing to the blue sky and scattered clouds.

I inhaled the clean, fresh air. A flock of geese flew over, honking, changing leaders like it was some kind of game. Crows cawed back and forth. To get to the stable, I had to trudge through snow that drifted to my waist. I couldn't imagine anybody driving in this.

Orphan nickered before I opened the stable door. I called to her, and she whinnied loud and long. I ran straight to her stall and said good morning. Cheyenne stuck her head over her stall door and let me stroke her jaw. "Sorry you had to spend the night with these fancy horses," I said. Both horses seemed edgy, but I figured Dalton Stables would do that to any horse.

Their water tanks had thin layers of ice over the surfaces. I broke the ice easily and went for oats.

"Can I help?" B.C. stood just inside the stable door. He'd either fallen down or rolled in the snow on purpose. "Stee-ven told me to leave so he could call *Hurl*-salad."

"Thanks. I can sure use the help, B.C.," I

said. "Each horse needs this much grain." I handed him a scoop and a measuring can. "And break up the ice in every water tank."

I stretched out my back, which had a kink in it from sleeping on the floor. "What I'd really like to do is set these prisoners free. I'll bet some of these horses have never even felt snow. I know Cheyenne and Orphan are itching to get outside. We can turn them out in the paddock as soon as we're finished with chores."

B.C. took the grain, frowning with concentration.

"Why don't you start at the far end, B.C.?" I said. "Check on that mare in the last stall. She was so restless yesterday I thought she might be close to having her foal. But Stephen says she's not."

I'd just sneaked in Champion's oats without getting bitten again, when B.C. let out a yell. "Yuk! Gross! Scoop, what's wrong with it? Hurry! Help!"

He was staring into the last stall, the thoroughbred broodmare's stall. I dropped my can of oats and raced down to him.

The mare was sweaty, but she also was waxing. A thick, yellowish liquid dripped down her hind legs. She lay down, then got back to her feet. Her head turned back to her stomach. Then she pawed the ground.

"Horsefeathers!" I cried, pulling B.C. out of the way. "That mare is having her baby!"

21

H elp her!" B.C. cried. "She's dying!"
"I can't help her!" I said. "I've never delivered a foal." The same fear I'd felt for Dotty and
for Jen seemed to jump at the chance to smother
me again. What if the mare really was dying?

"We have to call the vet!" I started for the
house, pushing B.C. ahead of me.

"We can't just leave her like that!" B.C.
shouted. "We can't leave her alone, Scoop. She'd
be a-scared."

He was right. I put my hand on his shoulder
and bent down to look him in the eyes. "Okay,
B.C. You can stay with her. Will you do that?"

He nodded.

"But she can't see you watching or she'll try
not to have the foal."

Hay bales were piled at the end of the stallway, making stairs almost to the ceiling. "Look,
B.C.," I whispered. "You can climb to that middle bale and scoot back so the mare can't see
you. Keep an eye on her. I'll call for help."

B.C. headed for the hay.

I raced out of the barn. It had been a long time since I'd seen a foal dropped, and my heart beat faster. Grandad never used to let me watch the births if he could help it.

Stephen was plodding down the hill just as I came racing up. We plowed into each other, knocking ourselves into the snow bank. I rolled halfway down the hill. "Stephen!" I yelled, struggling to my feet. "Got—to call the vet!"

"What's wrong?" He was brushing snow off his $500 coat. "I thought you wanted me to help—"

I climbed the hill again. "I'll call her."

"Call who?" he asked.

"Vicki Snyder. The vet?"

"You can't," he said.

"Don't get in my way!" I warned him.

"No, I mean you can't phone anybody. The lines are down or something."

"They can't be!" I said, terror making me want to vomit. My whole chest burned.

"Tell me about it," he said sullenly. "I was talking to Ursula, and we were just about to straighten things out when the line went dead. She probably thinks I hung up on her."

"Stephen," I said, "that mare is having her foal."

His eyes got bigger than I thought they could, almost the size of normal eyes. "She can't do that! The groom's not here!"

"Well you go tell her that then, Stephen, because somebody forgot to tell her she couldn't have her foal today." I thought of the story I'd told B.C. about Orphan only a few hours ago. I always skipped over the part about why we had to feed Orphan with the bottle, the part about how Orphan's mother had died giving birth to her.

"I'm going to try the phone," I said, pushing past him.

"Wait a minute!" Stephen cried. "What am I supposed to do?"

I tried to think. What did Grandad always do? For one thing, the mare needed to feel like she wasn't in a stone cold prison. "Give her a better bed, Stephen!" I called down. "Cover up all that sawdust and rubber stuff with hay, lots of hay! Then get out of her way."

Jen must have read the fear on my face the second I walked in. "What is it, Scoop? What's happened? Is it Cheyenne?"

I filled her in while I tried the phone. It was dead. *Dead*—I didn't even want to think the word. "What are we going to do?" I asked her.

Jen was already putting on her coat and boots. She winced as she pulled on the left boot over her bad ankle. "I've never helped with a foal delivery either," she said. "But I've watched a lot of my brothers be born. And I've read all about foaling."

"Jen—" Words caught in my throat. I felt

too afraid to even go back to the barn. I hadn't let go of the telephone. "You ... you can't mean us. We can't help."

"*I* can't," she said, pulling on gloves. "But you can. And I'll tell you everything I know. Most foals are dropped in the middle of the night without human help, Scoop. That mare may not need us at all. But she didn't have it in the night. And that makes me think something might not be quite right."

"What do you mean?" I asked, panic building. "What's not right?"

"We won't know until we go out there and try to help, will we?" Jen looked directly at me, not glancing away like she usually does. Her blue eyes cut through all my excuses. "Look, Scoop," she began. "I did a lot of thinking last night, and a lot of praying. I'm asking God to help me do what I need to do. Maybe that's what you need to do now too."

We didn't say anything else, but silently walked outside. With Jen leaning on me, we made our way to the stables. I tried to pray like Jen said, to ask God to help me do what I needed to do. But I was still scared. What if I did something wrong and the mare and foal died?

B.C. came running over to us before we got all the way inside the stable. "Help the horse, Scoop!" He was crying and breathing hard. "We made her a real nice bed, but she gets up and lies

176

down and gets up and—"

"That's all normal, B.C.," Jen said. "But we'll make her nervous if we all hover around her." Jen shifted her arm from around me to around B.C. "Let's find a place out of the way where we can keep an eye on her."

Stephen was in the hay perch above the stall, halfway up the stack of bales. With Stephen pulling and B.C. and me pushing, we got Jen up beside Stephen. Then B.C. joined them. So far the mare didn't seem to mind having me around, so I stayed close to the stall.

The mare jerked her head toward her flank as if somebody had just spurred her. She was covered in sweat and dripping milk now. She kicked at her belly as if a wasp had stung her there. Then her knees buckled and she plopped to her side.

A small sac that looked like a murky balloon came out of her. "That's the birth sac," Jen whispered. "She's having contractions. It won't be long now."

I couldn't tell where my fear left off and excitement began. Maybe this would just be a normal birth with nothing to worry about. I watched her belly contract. After a few minutes, watery liquid burst out, the fetal membrane.

The mare looked back at the liquid, amazed. She seemed puzzled, fascinated with it. She sniffed at it. Then she curled her upper lip and looked like she laughed. I heard B.C. laugh too.

Jen whispered to B.C. while we waited and the mare sniffed. "See her smelling it, B.C.?" Jen said. "That odor is how she'll identify her foal when it comes out. She'll be able to pick it out in pitch dark from hundreds of foals that look just alike to us."

"I think it's disgusting," Stephen said.

Not me. I felt an awe at this birth, a thankfulness that God would let us see it. Thankfulness! It was Thanksgiving Day! I wanted to shout "Happy Thanksgiving!" but I didn't want to upset the mare. So inside I just told God, *Happy Thanksgiving! And thanks!*

"Look!" B.C. cried. "It's a foot!"

Sure enough, one small hoof and the wet, brown foreleg poked its way out. I watched, my heart speeding up, waiting for the other hoof. It didn't come.

I looked up at Jen. Her neck was stretched out, and she looked worried too. In a normal foaling, both forelegs come out together, and the nose in between. I saw the tip of a nose, but still no right foreleg.

"Jen?" I cried, panicked, knowing this meant trouble. Big trouble. There is no way a foal can come out with one leg up and the other back. He could end up strangling himself and killing the mother too.

22

W e need a vet!" I looked around, half crazy, as if I'd find a vet hidden somewhere in the stables. "We have to have a vet! What are we going to do?"

"Scoop!" Jen said firmly. "Listen to me. You're going to have to help that mare."

God, I prayed, *I can't do this! What if I do something wrong? What if they die? What if they die because of me?* I looked up at Jen and shook my head. "I'm too afraid, Jen," I said.

"Then pray ... and trust, Scoop," she said. "Remember what B.C. said?"

"Me?" B.C. asked.

"That foal believes the only world it will ever see is that mare's little bitty womb. Are you going to help it see the world or not?"

This time when I prayed, I could almost feel God taking over, telling me not to be afraid. "Tell me what to do," I said.

Jen took on the role of major-general and barked commands to her troops. "Stephen, go to the house and get hot water. You'll have to hold

179

a bucket over the candles or kerosene lantern. Bring it out here. But first, get us plastic gloves, sleeves would be best, like the vet wears."

"The night groom keeps his stuff in the tack room," Stephen said, jumping down from the hay bales and racing off.

"We'll need soap, water, and disinfectant," Jen called after us.

We scurried like mad mice dodging a cat's paw. In minutes, we had everything collected. Stephen found a Bunsen burner, and the water heated fast. I scrubbed up with soap and water, then pulled the plastic gloves and sleeves on.

The mare groaned and stayed on her side, and the lone foot hung motionless from her. Jen told me how to scrub around the horse's opening and bandage her tail out of my way. The mare didn't even seem to notice I was there. Her only movements were head jerks looking back at her flanks. I knew she was in pain.

"Now what?" I asked, out of breath.

"Reach in for the other hoof," Jen said. "If we're lucky, it's there, but the foal just hasn't stuck it out yet."

My hands were shaking. I prayed God would steady me. Then I reached inside. I could feel the foal's nose. Then I touched something that felt like a hoof. "It's there!" I cried. "I feel it!"

"Now pull!" Jen commanded. "Pull it even with the other hoof."

I grabbed the little leg at the pastern, right above the hoof. Leaning in, I tugged and tugged. The foot moved, but I couldn't get it to the opening. "It won't come! I can't get it!" I tried with all my might, but it wouldn't fit through the opening.

"Are you sure?" Jen called. "Try, Scoop!"

I pulled so hard I felt light-headed. "It's no use." Then I had an idea. Grandad used to talk about his mares who dropped their foals standing up, like in the wild.

"Somebody help get this mare to her feet!" I shouted, not letting go of the foreleg.

"I'm not going in there," Stephen said. "Mares can go crazy over their foals. If she loses this one—"

"I'm coming!" Jen yelled, hobbling down the hay bales, B.C. at her side. At the stall, she told B.C. to stay out, and she slipped inside with me. "See if you can push back on this hoof while you pull out the other one," she said. "I'll try to help."

Groaning, the mare let us push her up. She stumbled and almost fell back down again, but finally, she was standing. I felt the foal move inside, the womb shift.

And it happened. The left foreleg went back inside, and I was able to pull the right one up even. With another yank, both legs came out together, the foal's fuzzy muzzle between.

"You did it!" Jen cried.

I was crying like a baby.

We watched as a perfect, dark chestnut filly dropped from her mother. The foal left her tiny world and came into ours with her eyes wide open. I wondered if Jen was thinking the same thing I was. And I wondered why a birth made death seem not so scary.

Beside me, Jen whispered, "Maybe, Scoop. Maybe."

I turned to her, knowing exactly what she meant. Maybe she'd tell her family everything about her symptoms. Maybe she'd trust God and do whatever she had to do to get well.

With our arms around each other, we watched as the gutsy filly tried to raise her head. Her mom bent her neck around and began licking her baby, nickering to her. Only a few minutes old, but that filly nickered back, a high, gravelly nicker than made us laugh. Their noses touched in a gentle gesture that made me want to cry again.

"You better cut that cord!" Stephen shouted as if he were suddenly in command.

"If that's the way you do it at Dalton Stables," Jen said, "you ought to tell them to stop it. Foals need everything that's inside their mothers, and they won't get it if you cut the cord for them. Her mother will take better care of that than we can."

Since the mare didn't mind having me

around, I stroked the filly and fingered her ears and hooves. I knew how important the first few hours of birth could be for a foal. Handling her now would make her life easier later. She'd remember a gentle touch and want to please her handler.

After a while, the mare stepped away, and the cord broke naturally. Jen made Stephen go to the house and bring out iodine. Then I sneaked up and put iodine on the foal's stump.

Jen sent Stephen to the house on so many errands, I suspected she was doing it just so she could hear him complain. He fetched bucket after bucket of warm water, which the mare drank gratefully.

The mare licked her foal's mouth and nose, then licked her all over. Meanwhile, the foal moved her mouth soundlessly. She tried to lift her head and forelegs up, but her mom nudged her back down, cleaning and cleaning.

After another hour, and dozens of failed attempts at standing, attempts that toppled the filly and sent us into fits of laughter, she stood all by herself. Her legs looked way too long to hold her up. She wobbled, ears twitching. It was almost another hour before she found her breakfast and started nursing.

"Can you believe that in one day," Jen said, "that newborn will already be able to walk, trot, canter, gallop—"

"And to think," I said to Stephen, "those things took you about 13 years to learn. Right, Stephen?"

"Very funny," Stephen answered, as if he didn't find it funny at all.

"Plus," Jen continued, "this little filly will be able to play, swim, roll—"

"Roll!" I raced from the stall. "Roll!" I yelled.

Stephen sighed. "What do you want me to get this time?"

"No," I said, bursting into Orphan's stall and leading her out, then doing the same for Cheyenne. "I'm setting the prisoners free!" I explained.

I unlatched every stall in Dalton Stables, even Champion's, and led them like a Thanksgiving parade out the door to the paddock. The sun made the paddock sparkle. Orphan took one look and tore out, kicking up snow as she playfully bucked. Cheyenne followed her, tossing her mane, rearing and snorting.

"Go on!" I told the rest of them. "The snow won't hurt you! It's fun! You know, *fun*?"

"Hey!" Stephen shouted. "You can't do that!"

The Arabian stepped out first, gingerly placing one foot into the snow, looking amazed when her hoof sank into the cold.

Then the rest followed her. Champion put his nose into the white fluffy stuff and blew, jerking his head up when the snow flew back in his face. Other horses snorted and made grunts and whinnies as they tried this new taste of freedom.

In minutes, they were all prancing like Orphan, racing the white fences, dancing to a music we couldn't hear, hooves stepping to the inaudible beat. It was horse music. I knew. I feel it sometimes when I ride Orphan and the wind is just right. Dotty calls it angel music, the kind you hear only in your head.

Through the open stable door, I could see the mare and foal standing—mother's neck arched over her filly, who pressed against her chest. The sun through the window behind them outlined their figures in gold dust.

Jen joined me and stared at the miracle foal. "Okay," she whispered. "I'll do what I need to do, what I need to live."

Thank You, I prayed, turning to hug Jen.

"Look!" B.C. screamed. "They're coming! They're coming!"

I squinted against the sun and saw what looked like a mirage, a line of figures coming our way. "Horsefeathers!" I muttered.

Stephen waved his arms like he was flagging down a rescue pilot. "Here! We're over here!"

"I think they know that, Stephen," Jen said. "That's Pastor Dan on a horse! And Maggie! Ray and Carla. And Travis! Somebody's driving a snowplow. There must be half a dozen horses."

I crossed the paddock for a better look. Orphan ran after me, and Cheyenne followed her.

"Quick, Stephen!" I hollered. "Run to the house!"

"What now?" he whined. "More water?"

"No!" I tried to sound as commanding as Jen. "Get an empty jar and bring it out here!"

"I don't know where any empty jars are," he complained.

"Then dump one out, wash it, and bring it here! Hurry!"

Stephen looked longingly at our rescuers, who were still far away, their voices barely reaching us. Then he took off for the house.

The paddock opened into a side pasture. I opened the gate, and the horses ran toward the mass of Thanksgiving rescuers. It was a Thanksgiving parade I'd never forget.

I could make out one of the volunteer firefighters driving the snowplow, clearing the path for snowmobiles and horses behind him. A tall, lean figure stuck his head out of the snowplow window. It had to be the firefighter, Wade Wilson.

Somebody else was leaning out of the cab of the snowplow, waving short arms. B.C. stared too. "Dotty!" he screamed, and tried to run to her. I ran too, and we tumbled in the snow, helping each other up.

And there was Travis, looking like an old-time cowboy on his Appaloosa. He whistled loud and waved. I waved back, and heard Jen whistle back from somewhere behind me. Maggie 37 stood in Moby's saddle and waved her cowboy hat.

Then they were all there with us—horses, friends, everybody I was most thankful for. Dotty and B.C. and I lost ourselves in a three-way hug.

Mr. Ford came up behind us. "You had us pretty worried," he said. "Did you know convicts were on the loose? They're back in jail now—stole a car and got it stuck in a snowdrift." He wore a plaid hunter's cap, with the flaps over his ears.

"Mr. Ford?" I said, staring at him, wondering if I'd ever seen him outside the Hy-Klas. "I hung up on you. I'm sorry."

"Scoop?" Dotty said. "Mr. Ford was calling to offer me my job back."

"He was?"

Mr. Ford grinned. "We didn't even last one hour without your aunt. I went back to the store for the receipts and found my niece and her friends partying—with *my* groceries."

"Gail Gayle?" I asked.

"I should have known." Mr. Ford shivered. "I'm sorry, Scoop."

I knew he meant he was sorry for thinking I was the shoplifter. "It's okay," I said, "as long as you're giving Dotty a raise." I winked at my aunt. "Right, Dotty?"

Dotty looked embarrassed. "I reckon that ain't such a bad idea."

Orphan let out a whinny so loud we all turned to look at her. Then as if she'd just issued a command and now planned to demonstrate for us, she dropped in the snow and rolled over on her back.

"Horse angels!" I cried, falling backward into the snow myself, spreading my wings.

B.C. plopped beside me and made his own snow angel. Then Dotty sat in the snow and leaned back, her short, thick legs making perfect angel swipes in the snow. All around me I heard the *plop, plop, plop* of people following Orphan's lead, covering the hillside with glittering snow angels.

Cheyenne hung her head above me. I looked up and begged her, "Come on, Cheyenne. Trust me. Make a horse angel." Inside I prayed. I held the Paint in my gaze, not looking away, praying to God for the horse to trust me. In slow motion, Cheyenne leaned forward in the snow, her knees touching the ground behind me. Then she bent her hindlegs and lay on top of the snow.

"That's it!" I cried. "Make a horse angel like Orphan."

Cheyenne nickered, then rolled over joyfully, her legs kicking in the air, her back twisting side to side, etching a snowy angel that could have put out any fire in the world.

Stephen stormed up to me, panting.

"Here's—your—jar." He doubled over and took in some deep breaths, then straightened up. "What's the matter with everybody? Why are they rolling in the snow? That jar better be important, Scoop. I had to dump out the caviar to get it. What's it for?"

Jen and Travis ran up to us. They were covered in snow. "I'll bet I know what the jar is for," Jen said. "And it *is* very important."

Jen knew. I needed Stephen's caviar jar for air. I was following my grandad's tradition of collecting the air from important moments of my life. Some people have photo albums or journals to help them remember. I have jars of air. This jar would remind me of the day that I realized the importance of God's gift of faith in Jesus.

Jen reached down and unscrewed the lid. God flooded my mind with His words, a passage from Psalm 27, "The Lord is my light and my salvation—whom shall I fear?" Suddenly the fears that had plagued me since Halloween melted like snowflakes in sunshine.

Travis helped me to my feet. I stood in the snow, holding the glass jar in both hands, and made a wide sweep above my head, as high as I could reach. I captured the scent of horses and snowflakes, the sounds of laughter and newborn nickers, air filled with friendship and trust and answered prayers, bursting with the silence of horse angel music and thanksgiving to God.

Foaling Facts

Terms for Horses

Mare—Female adult horse.

Stallion—An unaltered adult male horse.

Gelding—An altered male horse (can't be bred).

Sire—The father of a foal; foals are said to be *by* a certain stallion. The foal is his *get*.

Dam—The mother of a foal; foals are said to be *out of* a certain mare.

Foal—A newborn horse of either sex; foals are *foaled* or *dropped* (technically, rather than being "born").

Colt—A male horse from birth through three years old, if unaltered.

Filly—A female horse from birth through three years old, when she becomes a mare.

Normal Presentation—The usual way a foal is dropped from its dam: two front legs exit first, with the nose between.

Breech—"Backwards" birth, with the tail end coming out first and both rear legs stuck inside.

Waxing—The dam's milk dripping or streaming from the udders; usually a warning that her time is near, generally 12–24 hours away.

Placenta—The cleanings or afterbirth.